Mr Majeika

Humphrey Carpenter

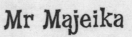

Mr Majeika

Mr Majeika
and the Lost
Spell Book

Illustrated by Frank Rodgers

PUFFIN

PUFFIN BOOKS

Published by the Penguin Group
Penguin Books Ltd, 80 Strand, London WC2R ORL, England
Penguin Group (USA) Inc., 375 Hudson Street, New York, New York 10014, USA
Penguin Group (Canada), 90 Eglinton Avenue East, Suite 700, Toronto, Ontario, Canada M4P 2Y3
(a division of Pearson Penguin Canada Inc.)
Penguin Ireland, 25 St Stephen's Green, Dublin 2, Ireland (a division of Penguin Books Ltd)
Penguin Group (Australia), 707 Collins Street, Melbourne, Victoria 3008, Australia
(a division of Pearson Australia Group Pty Ltd)
Penguin Books India Pvt Ltd, 11 Community Centre, Panchsheel Park, New Delhi – 110 017, India
Penguin Group (NZ), 67 Apollo Drive, Rosedale, Auckland 0632, New Zealand
(a division of Pearson New Zealand Ltd)
Penguin Books (South Africa) (Pty) Ltd, Block D, Rosebank Office Park, 181 Jan Smuts Avenue,
Parktown North, Gauteng 2193, South Africa

Penguin Books Ltd, Registered Offices: 80 Strand, London WC2R ORL, England

puffinbooks.com

Mr Majeika first published by Kestrel Books 1984
Published in Puffin Books 1985
Mr Majeika and the Lost Spell Book published by Puffin Books 2003
This edition published 2014
001

Mr Majeika text copyright © Humphrey Carpenter, 1984
Mr Majeika illustrations copyright © Frank Rodgers, 1984
Mr Majeika and the Lost Spell Book text copyright © Humphrey Carpenter, 2003
Mr Majeika and the Lost Spell Book illustrations copyright © Frank Rodgers, 2003
All rights reserved

The moral right of the author and illustrator has been asserted

Set in Palatino
Printed in Great Britain by Clays Ltd, St Ives plc

British Library Cataloguing in Publication Data
A CIP catalogue record for this book is available from the British Library

ISBN: 978-0-141-35081-3

www.greenpenguin.co.uk

Mr Majeika

With thanks to Class 7 at Marlborough Primary School, Chelsea, for their help, and especially Lucy Tsancheva, who thought of most of Chapters 7 and 8.

Contents

1. The Carpet-Bicycle

It was Monday morning, it was pouring with rain, and it was everyone's first day back at St Barty's Primary School after the Christmas holidays. That's why Class Three were in a bad temper.

Pandora Green had been rude to Melanie, so Melanie was crying (though Melanie always found *something* to cry about). Hamish Bigmore was trying to pick a quarrel with Thomas and Pete, the twins. And Mr Potter the head teacher was very cross because the new teacher for Class Three hadn't turned up.

'I can't think where he is,' he grumbled at Class Three. 'He should have been here at nine o'clock for the beginning of school. And now it's nearly ten, and I should be teaching Class Two. We'll have to open the folding doors and let you share the lesson with them.'

Class Three groaned. They thought themselves very important people, and didn't in the least want to share a lesson with Class Two, who were just babies.

'Bother this thing,' muttered Mr Potter, struggling with the folding doors that separated the classrooms.

'I'll help you, Mr Potter,' said Hamish Bigmore, who didn't really want to help at all, but just to be a nuisance as usual. And then everyone else began to shout: 'Don't let

Hamish Bigmore do it, he's no good, let *me* help,' so that in a moment there was uproar.

But suddenly silence fell. And there was a gasp.

Mr Potter was still fiddling with the folding doors, so he didn't see what was happening. But Class Three did.

One of the big windows in the classroom slid open all by itself, and *something* flew in.

It was a man on a magic carpet.

There could be no doubt about that. Class Three knew a magic carpet when they saw one. After all, they'd read *Aladdin* and all that sort of stuff. There are magic carpets all over the place in *Aladdin*. But this wasn't *Aladdin*. This was St Barty's Primary School on a wet Monday morning. And magic carpets don't turn up in schools. Class Three knew that. So they stared.

The carpet hung in the air for a moment, as if it wasn't sure what to do. Then it came down on the floor with a bump. 'Ow!' said the man sitting on it.

He was quite old, and he had a pointed beard and very bright eyes, behind a pair of glasses. His hair and clothes were wet from the rain. On the whole he looked quite ordinary – except for the fact that he was sitting on a magic carpet.

'I just can't manage it,' said Mr Potter, still pushing at the folding doors. 'I'll have to go and get the caretaker.'

Then he saw the man on the carpet.

'What – how – eh?' said Mr Potter. Words usually deserted Mr Potter at difficult moments.

The man on the carpet scrambled to his feet. 'Majeika,' he said politely, offering his hand.

Mr Potter took the hand. 'Majeika?' he repeated, puzzled. Then a look of understanding dawned on his face. 'Ah,' he said, 'Mr Majeika!' He turned to Class Three. 'Boys and girls,' he said, 'I want you to meet Mr Majeika. He's your new teacher.'

For a moment there was silence. Then Melanie began to cry: 'Boo-hoo! I'm *frightened* of him! He came on a magic carpet!'

'What's the matter, Melanie?' snapped Mr Potter. 'I can't hear a word you're saying. It sounded like "magic carpet" or some such nonsense.' He turned briskly to Mr Majeika. 'Now, you're rather late, Mr Majeika. You might have telephoned me.'

'I'm so sorry,' said Mr Majeika. 'You see, my magic carpet took a wrong turning. It's normally quite good at finding the way, but I think the rain must have got into it. I do beg your pardon.'

'Never mind,' said Mr Potter. 'And now . . . Wait a minute, did I hear you say *magic carpet*?'

It was Mr Majeika's turn to look bothered. 'Oh, did I really say that? How very silly of me. A complete slip of the tongue. I meant – *bicycle*, of course. I came on a bicycle.'

'Quite so,' said Mr Potter. 'Bicycle, of course . . .' His voice tailed off. He was staring at the magic carpet. 'What's that?' he said rather faintly.

'That?' said Mr Majeika cheerily. 'That's

my magic –' He cleared his throat. 'Oh dear, my mistake again. *That's my bicycle.*' And as he said these last words, he pointed a finger at the magic carpet.

There was a funny sort of humming noise, and the carpet rolled itself up and turned into a bicycle.

Mr Majeika leant cheerily against the handlebars and rang the bicycle bell. 'Nice bike, isn't it?' he said, smiling at Mr Potter.

You could have heard a pin drop.

Mr Potter turned rather white. 'I – I don't think I feel very well,' he said at last. 'I – I don't seem to be able to tell the difference between a carpet and a bicycle.'

Mr Majeika smiled even more cheerily. 'Never mind, a very easy mistake to make. And now I think it's time I began to teach our young friends here.'

Mr Potter wiped his forehead with his handkerchief. 'What? Oh – yes – of course,' he muttered faintly, backing to the door. 'Yes, yes, please do begin. Can't tell a bicycle from a carpet . . .' he mumbled to himself as he left the room.

'Now then,' said Mr Majeika to Class Three, 'to work!'

2. Chips for Everyone

Never had Class Three been so quiet as they were for the rest of that lesson. They sat in absolute silence as Mr Majeika told them what work he planned to give them for the rest of that term.

Not that any of them was really listening to what he was saying. It actually sounded very ordinary, with stuff about nature-study, and the kings and queens of England, and special projects, and that sort of thing, just like all the other teachers. But they couldn't take it in. Each of them was thinking about just one thing: the magic carpet.

When break came, and they were all having milk and biscuits, they whispered about it.

'I *saw* it,' whispered Pandora Green's best friend Jody.

'So did I,' said Thomas and Pete together. 'It *was* a magic carpet.'

'If you ask *me*,' said Hamish Bigmore, 'it was a mass hallucination.' Hamish Bigmore was always learning long words just so that he could show them off.

'What's that mean?' said Thomas and Pete suspiciously.

'It's when you think you've seen something and you haven't,' said Hamish Bigmore. 'People get them when they're walking across the desert. They think they see a pool of water, and when they get there, there's only sand.'

'But we're not in the desert, you idiot,' said Thomas. 'And we didn't see water, we saw a magic carpet, and it turned into a bicycle. And we *all* saw it, so how could we have imagined it?'

'That's why it's called *mass* hallucination,' said Hamish Bigmore grandly. '*Mass* means lots of people. So idiot yourself!'

And they might have believed him, if it wasn't for what happened at dinner.

Most of Class Three ate school dinner, but some of them were sent to school with packed lunches which their mothers had made at home, and which they ate at a separate table. Thomas and Pete did this, and so did Jody.

So did Wim. He was Thomas and Pete's younger brother. He was in the nursery class, so Thomas and Pete only saw him at dinner time. He was really called William, but 'Wim' was how he said his own name, so that was what everyone called him.

Wim was tucking happily into a piece of egg and bacon flan, which was his favourite lunch. Thomas and Pete were talking to Jody while they ate theirs. 'What do you think about the magic carpet?' they asked her for the hundredth time.

'Ssh, here he comes!' whispered Jody.

Mr Majeika was approaching their table. He sat down next to them. 'Hello,' he said in a friendly manner. 'Was there anything you wanted to ask me about the lessons for this term?'

Thomas, Pete and Jody looked at each other. Of course there was something they wanted to ask him!

Suddenly there was a wail from Wim. He had dropped his egg and bacon flan on the floor.

Thomas and Pete looked gloomily at each other. They would have to give Wim some of their own dinner.

'My poor chap, most unfortunate,' said Mr Majeika. He bent down and picked up the mess of egg and bacon flan. 'We must see what we can do with this,' he said to Wim. 'Tell me, my young friend, what is your favourite food?'

Wim thought for a moment. Then he said: 'Chips.'

'Ah,' said Mr Majeika, shutting his eyes

for a moment, and pointing at Wim's plate. 'Chips.'

'Oo!' said Wim suddenly. And no wonder, for on his plate, where the broken bits of flan had been, stood a huge pile of steaming hot chips.

'Oh!' said Thomas, Pete and Jody.

'Would you like some too, my young friends?' said Mr Majeika. Thomas, Pete and Jody nodded, and suddenly, out of nowhere, there were piles of chips on their plates too.

'Gosh!' said Thomas, Pete and Jody.

Suddenly another voice broke in. 'What's this? You know we don't allow chips here at dinner time.' It was Mr Potter.

He had come up behind Mr Majeika without anyone noticing. 'It's a very strict rule,' he said. 'Parents may send their children to school with sandwiches or other cold food, but I will not allow boys and girls

to go out and buy chips during the dinner hour.'

'But we didn't buy them,' began Thomas.

'No, no,' interrupted Mr Majeika quickly. 'They certainly didn't buy them. It was *I* who provided them, not knowing the school rules. It won't happen again.'

'Well,' said Mr Potter crossly, 'please don't let it.' He walked off.

Mr Majeika sighed. 'Oh dear,' he said, 'I think I've got a lot to learn in my new job.

You see, I'm not at all experienced at being a teacher. I've always worked as, well . . . something else.'

Thomas hesitated for a moment, then plucked up courage to say: 'Do you mean you were a *wizard*?'

Mr Majeika nodded. 'I might as well admit it,' he said. 'I worked as one for years, but then I began to get a bit rusty on my spells, and recently there hasn't been much business. People don't believe much in wizards nowadays, so naturally they don't often pay them to do some work. So in the end I just had to get another kind of job. That's why I'm here. And now I really *must* remember that I'm a teacher, and not a wizard at all. And you must all help me. You mustn't try to persuade me to do any –' He hesitated.

'Any magic?' said Pete.

Mr Majeika nodded. 'You must let me be an *ordinary teacher*,' he said. 'Do you promise?'

They all nodded. But each of them thought it would be a very difficult promise to keep.

*

By three-fifteen that day, when afternoon school was nearly at an end, nothing else out of the ordinary had happened in Class Three. In fact the afternoon would have ended very boringly if it hadn't been for Hamish Bigmore.

Hamish had been put to sit next to Melanie, which was a bad thing for Melanie, as Hamish liked nothing better than to make her cry.

Sure enough, when there were only a few more minutes to go, Melanie started to sob. 'Boo-hoo! Hamish Bigmore is jabbing me with his ruler!'

Hamish Bigmore said he wasn't, but Mr Majeika moved fast enough to get to the scene of the crime before Hamish had time to hide the ruler. 'Put it down!' said Mr Majeika.

'Shan't,' said Hamish Bigmore.

There was silence, and everyone in Class Three remembered how Hamish Bigmore had refused to do as he was told by last term's teacher. It was mostly because of him that she had left the school.

'Put it down,' said Mr Majeika again.

'Shan't,' said Hamish Bigmore for a second time.

'Then,' said Mr Majeika slowly, '*I shall make you wish very much that you had put it down.*'

And Hamish Bigmore screamed.

'A snake! Help! Help!' he shouted. And there fell from his hand something that certainly wasn't a ruler.

It was a long grey-green snake with patterned markings and a forked tongue. Its mouth was open and it was hissing.

In a moment everyone else was shouting too, and clambering on to the desks, and doing anything they could to get out of its reach. But not Mr Majeika.

He stepped calmly up to the snake, knelt down, and picked it up. And as his hand touched it, it turned back into a ruler.

'What are you frightened of?' he asked Hamish Bigmore. 'This is only your ruler.

But perhaps next time you will do as you are told.'

He gave the ruler back to Hamish Bigmore, who dropped it fearfully on his desk and shrank away from it.

A moment later the bell rang, and school was over for the day. Class Three usually rushed outside as soon as they heard the bell. But today they were quiet as mice.

'He *said* he didn't want to do any magic,' said Thomas to Pete on the way home.

'I think he just forgets about that now and then,' said Pete. 'After all, if you've been a wizard for years, it can't be easy stopping overnight.'

'Mr Majeika . . .' said Thomas thoughtfully to himself. 'Do you know, I don't think that's his real name.'

'No,' said Pete. 'I think he ought to be called Mr Magic.'

3. Hamish Goes Swimming

In fact for a long time after that Mr Magic, as all Class Three were soon calling him, *didn't* forget that he was meant to be a teacher, and not a wizard. Nothing peculiar happened for weeks and weeks, and the lessons went on just as they would have with any other teacher. The magic carpet, the chips, and the snake seemed like a dream.

Then Hamish Bigmore came to stay at Thomas and Pete's house.

This wasn't at all a good thing, at least not for Thomas and Pete. But they had no choice. Hamish Bigmore's mother and father had to go away for a few days, and Thomas and Pete's mum had offered to look after Hamish until they came back. She never asked Thomas and Pete what they thought about the idea until it was too late.

Hamish Bigmore behaved even worse than they had expected. He found all their favourite books and games, which they had tried to hide from him, and spoilt them or left them lying about the house where they got trodden on and broken. He pulled the stuffing out of Wim's favourite teddy bear, bounced up and down so hard on the garden climbing-frame that it bent, and talked for hours and hours after the light had been put out at night, so that Thomas and Pete couldn't get to sleep. 'It's awful,' said Thomas. 'I wish that something really nasty would happen to him.'

And it did.

Hamish Bigmore was behaving just as badly at school as at Thomas and Pete's house. The business of the ruler turning into a snake had frightened him for a few days, but no longer than that, and now he was up to his old tricks again, doing anything rather than listen to Mr Majeika and behave properly.

On the Wednesday morning before Hamish Bigmore's mother and father were due to come home, Mr Majeika was giving Class Three a nature-study lesson, with the tadpoles in the glass tank that sat by his desk. Hamish Bigmore was being ruder than ever.

'Does anyone know how long tadpoles take to turn into frogs?' Mr Majeika asked Class Three.

'Haven't the slightest idea,' said Hamish Bigmore.

'Please,' said Melanie, holding up her hand, 'I don't think it's very long. Only a few weeks.'

'*You* should know,' sneered Hamish Bigmore. 'You look just like a tadpole yourself.'

Melanie began to cry.

'Be quiet, Hamish Bigmore,' said Mr Majeika. 'Melanie is quite right. It all happens very quickly. The tadpoles grow arms and legs, and very soon –'

'I shouldn't think they'll grow at all if they see *you* staring in at them through the glass,' said Hamish Bigmore to Mr Majeika. 'Your face would frighten them to death!'

'Hamish Bigmore, I have had enough of you,' said Mr Majeika. 'Will you stop behaving like this?'

'No, I won't!' said Hamish Bigmore.

Mr Majeika pointed a finger at him.

And Hamish Bigmore vanished.

There was complete silence. Class Three stared at the empty space where Hamish Bigmore had been sitting.

Then Pandora Green pointed at the glass tank, and began to shout: 'Look! Look! A frog! A frog! One of the tadpoles has turned into a frog!'

Mr Majeika looked closely at the tank. Then he put his head in his hands. He seemed very upset.

'No, Pandora,' he said. 'It isn't one of the tadpoles. It's Hamish Bigmore.'

For a moment, Class Three were struck dumb. Then everyone burst out laughing. 'Hooray! Hooray! Hamish Bigmore has been turned into a frog! Good old Mr Magic!'

'It looks like Hamish Bigmore, doesn't it?' Pete said to Thomas. Certainly the frog's expression looked very much like Hamish's face. And it was splashing noisily around the tank and carrying on the silly sort of way that Hamish did.

Mr Majeika looked very worried. 'Oh dear, oh dear,' he kept saying.

'Didn't you mean to do it?' asked Jody.

Mr Majeika shook his head. 'Certainly not. I quite forgot myself. It was a complete mistake.'

'Well,' said Thomas, 'you can turn him back again, can't you?'

Mr Majeika shook his head again. 'I'm not at all sure that I can,' he said.

Thomas and Pete looked at him in astonishment.

'You see,' he went on, 'it was an old spell, something I learnt years and years ago and thought I'd forgotten. I don't know what were the exact words I used. And, as I am sure you understand, it's not possible to undo a spell unless you know exactly what the words were.'

'So Hamish Bigmore may have to stay a

frog?' said Pete. 'That's the best thing I've heard for ages!'

Mr Majeika shook his head. 'For you, maybe, but not for him. I'll have to try and do *something*.' And he began to mutter a whole series of strange-sounding words under his breath.

All kinds of things began to happen. The room went dark, and the floor seemed to rock. Green smoke came out of an empty jar on Mr Majeika's desk. He tried some more words, and this time there was a small thunderstorm in the sky outside. But nothing happened to the frog.

'Oh, dear,' sighed Mr Majeika, 'what *am* I going to do?'

4. The Frog's Princess

Thomas and Pete thought for a moment. Then Thomas said: 'Don't worry about it yet, Mr Magic. Hamish Bigmore's parents are away, and he's staying with us. You've got two days to find the right spell before they come back and expect to find him.'

'Two days,' repeated Mr Majeika. 'In that case there is a chance. We shall simply have to see what happens at midnight.'

'Midnight?' asked Jody.

'My friend,' said Mr Majeika, 'surely you know that in fairy stories everything returns to its proper shape when the clock strikes twelve?'

'Cinderella's coach,' said Jody.

'Exactly,' answered Mr Majeika. 'But one can't be certain of it. There's only a chance. I'll stay here tonight, and see what happens.'

And with that, Class Three went home.

Thomas and Pete felt that really they should have taken Hamish Bigmore home with them, even if he *was* a frog. After all, he was supposed to be staying with them.

'But,' said Pete, 'it's not easy carrying frogs. He might escape, and jump into a river or something, and we'd never see him again.'

'And a very good thing too,' said Thomas.

'You can't say that,' remarked Pete. 'He may be only Hamish Bigmore to you and me, but to his mum and dad he's darling little Hamie, or something like that. And just think what it would be like to be mother and father to a frog. Going to the shops, and the library, and that sort of thing, and people saying: "Oh, Mrs Bigmore, what a *sweet* little frog you're carrying in that jar." And Hamish's mum having to say: "Oh, Mrs Smith, that's not just a frog, that's our son Hamish."'

When Thomas and Pete's mum saw them at the school gates the first thing she said was 'Where's Hamish?', and they had quite a time persuading her that Hamish wouldn't be coming home with them that afternoon, or staying the night, but was visiting friends, and was being perfectly well taken care of.

'Who are these friends?' she asked suspiciously. 'What's their name?'

'Tadpoles,' said Pete, without thinking.

'Idiot,' whispered Thomas, kicking him. 'We don't know their name,' he told his mum. 'But Mr Majeika, our new teacher, arranged it, so it must be all right.'

'Oh, did he?' said their mum. 'Well, he might have told me. But I suppose I shouldn't fuss.' And she took them home.

When they got back to school the next morning, Hamish Bigmore was still a frog.

'Nothing happened at all,' said Mr
Majeika gloomily.

He tried to make Class Three get on with
their ordinary work, but it wasn't much use.
Nobody had their minds on anything but
Hamish Bigmore, swimming up and down in
his tank.

Everyone kept making suggestions to Mr
Majeika.

'Mr Magic, couldn't you just get a magic
wand and wave it over him?'

'Couldn't you say "Abracadabra" and see
if that works?'

'Couldn't you find another wizard and ask
him what to do?'

'My friends,' said Mr Majeika, 'it's no use.
There's nothing else to try. Last night, while
I was here alone, I made use of every
possible means I know, and I can do
nothing. And as to finding another wizard,

that would be very hard indeed. There are so very few still working, and we don't know each other's names. It might take me years to find another one, and even then he might not have the answer.'

Class Three went home rather gloomily that day. They had all begun to feel sorry for Hamish Bigmore. 'He's staying with his friends again,' Thomas and Pete told their mother.

The next day was Friday. Hamish Bigmore's parents were due to come home that evening.

Half-way through morning school, Jody suddenly put up her hand and said: 'Mr Magic?'

'Yes, Jody?'

'Mr Magic, I've got an idea. You said that things *sometimes* happen like they do in fairy stories. I mean, like Cinderella's coach turning back into a pumpkin.'

'Yes, sometimes,' said Mr Majeika, 'but as you've seen with Hamish, not always.'

'Well,' said Jody, 'there is something that I wondered about. You see, in fairy stories people are often turned into frogs. And they always get turned back again in the end, don't they? And I've been trying to remember *how*.'

Jody paused. 'Go on,' said Mr Majeika.

'Well,' said Jody, 'I *did* remember. Frogs turn back into princes when they get kissed by a princess.'

Mr Majeika's eyes lit up. 'Goodness!' he said. 'You're absolutely right! Why didn't I think of that? We must try it at once!'

'Try what, Mr Magic?' asked Pandora Green.

'Why, have Hamish Bigmore kissed by a princess. And then I do believe there's a very good chance he will change back.'

'But please, Mr Magic,' said Thomas, 'how are you going to manage it? I mean, there's not so very many princesses around these days. Not as many as in fairy stories.'

'There's some at Buckingham Palace,' said Pandora.

'But they don't go around kissing frogs,' said Thomas.

'You bet they don't,' said Pete. 'You see pictures of them in the newspapers doing all sorts of things, opening new hospitals, and naming ships, and that sort of thing. But not kissing frogs.'

'Are you sure, my young friend?' said Mr Majeika gloomily.

'Quite sure,' said Thomas. 'Unless they do it when nobody's looking. I mean, it's not the sort of thing they'd get much fun out of, is it? Frog-kissing, I mean.'

'I bet,' said Pete, 'that a real live princess wouldn't do it if you paid her a thousand pounds.'

'Just imagine,' said Thomas, 'going to Buckingham Palace, and ringing the doorbell, and saying: "Please, have you got any princesses in today, and would they mind kissing a frog for us?" They'd probably fetch the police.'

'Oh dear,' said Mr Majeika. 'I'm afraid you're right.'

Nobody spoke for a long time. Then Mr Majeika said gloomily: 'It seems that Hamish Bigmore will have to remain a frog. I wonder what his parents will say.'

'Please,' said Jody, 'I've got an idea again. It may be silly, but it *might* work. What I think is this. If we can't get a real princess, we might *pretend* to have one. Make a kind of play, I mean. Dress up somebody like a princess. Do you think that's silly?' She looked hopefully at Mr Majeika.

'Not at all,' said Mr Majeika. 'We've nothing to lose by trying it!'

Which was how Class Three came to spend a good deal of the morning trying to make the room look like a royal palace in a fairy story. They found the school caretaker and persuaded him to lend them some old blue curtains that were used for the play at the end of term. And Mrs Honey who taught the nursery class agreed to give them a box of dressing-up clothes that the little children used. In this were several crowns and robes and other things that could be made to look royal.

Then there was a dreadful argument about who was to play the princess.

Jody said she ought to, because it had all been her idea. Pandora Green said *she*

should, because she looked pretty, and
princesses always look pretty. Mr Majeika
tried to settle it by saying that Melanie
should do it, as she was the only girl in the
class who hadn't asked to. But Melanie, who
hated the idea of kissing a frog, started to
cry. So in the end Mr Majeika said that Jody
should do it after all, and the other girls
could be sort-of-princesses too, only Jody
would play the chief one.

Then they got ready. A kind of throne had
been made out of Mr Majeika's chair, with
one of the blue curtains draped over it.

Jody wore another of the curtains as a cloak, and one of the crowns, and a lot of coloured beads from the dressing-up box. And all the other girls stood round her.

Mr Majeika turned out the classroom lights and drew the curtains. Then he said he thought they ought to have some music, just to make things seem more like a fairy story. So Thomas got out his recorder, and played 'God Save the Queen' and 'Good King Wenceslas', which were the only tunes he knew. They didn't seem quite right for the occasion, but Mr Majeika said they would have to do. Then he told Jody to start being the princess, and say the sort of things that princesses might say in fairy stories.

Jody thought for a moment. Then she said in a high voice: 'O my courtiers, I have heard that in this kingdom there is a poor prince who has been enchanted into a frog by some wicked magician.' She turned to Mr Majeika and whispered: 'You're not wicked, really, Mr Magic, but that's what happens in fairy stories, isn't it?'

'Of course,' said Mr Majeika. 'Please continue. You are doing splendidly.'

'O my courtiers,' went on Jody, 'I do request that one of you shall speedily bring me this frog. For I have seen it written that should a princess of the blood royal kiss this poor frog with her own lips, he will regain his proper shape.' She paused. 'Well, go on, somebody,' she hissed. 'Fetch me the frog!'

It was Mr Majeika himself who stepped up to the tank, put in his hands, and drew out Hamish Bigmore. So he did not see the door opening and Mr Potter coming into the room.

'Ah, Mr Majeika,' said Mr Potter, 'I just wanted to ask you if you could look after school dinner again today, because –' He stopped, staring at the extraordinary scene.

Mr Majeika was kneeling on one knee in front of Jody, holding out the frog. 'Go on,' he whispered, 'I feel the magic working.'

'O frog,' said Jody in her high voice, 'O frog, I command you, turn back into a prince!' And she kissed the frog.

'Now, really,' said Mr Potter, 'I'm not at all in favour of nature-study being mixed up with story-times. And school curtains should not be used for this sort of thing. While as to that frog, its proper place is a pond. I'll allow tadpoles in school, but not frogs. They jump out of the tanks and get all over the place. Now, if you'll just hand that one over . . . Where is it?'

'Here I am,' said Hamish Bigmore. He had appeared out of nowhere, and the frog was gone.

Mr Potter sat down very suddenly in the nearest chair. 'I don't feel very well,' he said.

'Ah,' said Hamish Bigmore, 'you should try being a frog for a few days. Does you no end of good. Makes you feel really healthy, I can tell you. All that swimming about, why, I've never felt better in my life. And being kissed by princesses, too. Not that my princess was a real one.' He turned to Mr Majeika. 'You really should have taken me to Buckingham Palace,' he said. 'I'm sure the Queen herself would have done it, to oblige me.'

Mr Potter got to his feet and left the room, muttering something about needing to go and see a doctor because he was imagining things.

'And now,' said Hamish Bigmore to Class Three, 'I'm going to tell you all about the life and habits of the frog.' Which he did, at great length.

'Oh dear,' said Pete to Thomas. 'He's worse than ever.'

5. The Disappearing Bottle

It was about three weeks after this that several of Class Three went to see a film about Superman.

'The best bit,' said Jody to Pete and Thomas, 'was when he flew right over those tall buildings. I'd love to be able to fly like that. Do you think people ever can?'

'I shouldn't have thought so,' said Pete. 'But you could ask Mr Magic. I'm sure he'd know.'

So, when Class Three were beginning their next lesson, Jody did ask him: 'Mr Magic, can you really fly, like Superman?'

Mr Majeika smiled at her over his glasses.

'If you mean *me*, then certainly not! I'm too old for such things. But someone a bit younger could manage it, with a little help.'

'Do you mean a little magic?' asked Jody. Mr Majeika nodded.

'Rubbish!' shouted Hamish Bigmore. 'You couldn't make *anyone* fly, Mr Magic. No one could. It's scientifically impossible.' Since the business of the frog, Hamish Bigmore had been behaving worse than ever. Obviously he thought Mr Majeika wouldn't dare to do anything else to him.

Mr Majeika sighed wearily. 'It is not rubbish, Hamish Bigmore, but I don't intend to waste time showing you.'

'Oh do, please *do*,' said Jody, and soon there was a chorus of: 'Yes, *do*, Mr Magic! Couldn't you, just *once*?'

'Of course he can't,' sneered Hamish Bigmore.

'Very well then,' snapped Mr Majeika, 'just to prove Hamish Bigmore wrong, I will. But it will have to wait until tomorrow, when I can bring the potion.'

Everyone fell silent, wondering what 'the potion' was.

When the next day came, Mr Majeika seemed at first to have forgotten all about his promise, for he said nothing about it. At last Jody asked him: 'Did you bring the flying potion, Mr Magic?'

Mr Majeika frowned. 'Well, yes, I did. But really I think the whole idea is a mistake. I'd much rather we forgot all about it. These things have a way of getting out of hand . . .'

'There you are!' jeered Hamish Bigmore. 'I told you he couldn't do it.'

'Oh, really, Hamish Bigmore, you're enough to try the patience of a witch's broomstick,' grumbled Mr Majeika. 'I suppose I'll *have* to do it just to keep you quiet.'

'Do what, Mr Magic?' asked Thomas.

'Why, give you all some of the flying potion,' said Mr Majeika.

There was a happy uproar. 'What, all of us?' asked Pete. 'Are we all going to be able to fly?'

'Well, it'll have to be all or none,' answered Mr Majeika. 'Can you imagine how jealous everyone would be if I only let one or two of you do it? But it won't be proper flying, mind. Just a little hover in the air. The potion is far too precious to be wasted.'

Class Three tried to make him change his mind and allow them to fly properly, but he wouldn't. So in the end they queued up, and were each given a very small spoonful by Mr Majeika. It was green and sticky, and tasted like a rather nice cough mixture. Only

Hamish Bigmore refused to have any; he said the whole idea was silly.

As soon as they had taken it, Class Three began to jump up and down, in the hope of taking off into the air. But nothing happened.

They were all dreadfully disappointed. 'There you are!' sneered Hamish Bigmore. 'I told you so! It doesn't work!'

'Oh, but it does,' said Mr Majeika. 'I forgot to tell you that it takes exactly half an hour before anything happens. So we must get on with the lesson for the next half hour, and *then* see.'

It was a very long, slow half hour, and even when it ended nothing happened to Class Three. 'What's gone wrong?' Jody asked Mr Majeika.

'Nothing,' answered Mr Majeika, smiling. 'You can't just sit there and expect to fly without *doing* anything.'

'Do you mean we should wave our arms about or something?' asked Pete.

Mr Majeika shook his head. 'No, my friend. The secret is to *think* about flying. If the notion of flying comes into your head, then – hey presto!'

'I'm thinking hard about it,' said Jody. 'I'm thinking about floating up in the air from my desk, and – Oh! *Oh!*' Suddenly she found herself doing just that.

In a moment they were all doing it. It was a very peculiar feeling; you simply had to think about leaving the ground, and you did. What's more, once you were in the air, if you thought about (say) spinning round like a top, you found yourself doing it. Pete said:

'I'm going to think about floating across the room to the door –' and there he was, doing just that.

The only thing that disappointed them was that they were never very far from the floor. 'Can't you let us go higher?' they pleaded with Mr Majeika.

He shook his head. 'Too risky,' he said. 'You might bump your heads on the ceiling, or do all kinds of dreadful things. And anyway, I want to save my precious flying potion. It always wears off in half an hour, however much you take, so it would be an awful waste to give you lots of it.'

Alas, it did wear off in half an hour, to everyone's regret, and all too soon they were down on the ground again, quite unable to float, however much they thought about it.

'Well, my friends,' said Mr Majeika, 'I hope you enjoyed that. And,' he turned to Hamish Bigmore, who had been sitting watching everyone else float through the air, 'I hope *you* believe me now.'

'Oh yes, Mr Magic,' answered Hamish Bigmore, with a rather peculiar smile on his face.

'Very good,' said Mr Majeika. 'Well then, let me put the potion away, and we can get on again with our proper lessons, which today –' He stopped suddenly. 'What's happened to the potion?' he said.

The bottle had vanished.

'*Where is the potion?*' said Mr Majeika again, in an anxious voice. 'It was on my desk. Someone has picked it up and hidden it. Will they please return it at once?'

No one said anything. Mr Majeika turned to Hamish Bigmore. 'Hamish,' he said, 'somehow I have a feeling that *you* are behind this.'

Hamish Bigmore shook his head. 'Oh, no, Mr Majeika,' he said sweetly, 'why should *I* do a thing like that?'

Mr Majeika looked at him steadily. 'Turn out your pockets,' he said to Hamish. But the bottle wasn't in Hamish's pockets.

After that, Mr Majeika searched everyone in Class Three, saying as he did so: 'Oh dear, I *knew* I shouldn't have brought the potion to school. One of you has played a wretched trick on me, and it's quite unfair.'

'Perhaps,' suggested Hamish Bigmore, 'the bottle itself can fly, and it's flown away?' He laughed uproariously, but Mr Majeika was not amused.

Nowhere could the bottle be found, and

by the end of school for that day Mr Majeika was looking very worried and very cross.

'I'm sure it *is* Hamish,' said Pete to Thomas. 'He had something tucked under his coat when he left the classroom.'

'Well,' said Thomas, 'I'm sure we'll find out who's got it. Whoever they are, they're bound to start flying pretty soon.'

6. *Mr Potter Goes for a Spin*

But no one did. Days went by, then several weeks, and nothing peculiar happened in Class Three. After a time Mr Majeika, who at first had continued to look very worried and cross, stopped seeming to be so unhappy about the loss of his potion. Eventually he seemed to have forgotten all about it.

The weather gradually began to warm up. One morning, about two weeks before the end of term, it was so hot that Mr Majeika opened the windows in Class Three. For some reason Hamish Bigmore seemed very pleased at this, though no one could make out why.

Mr Majeika was in charge of school dinner that day, and he walked up and down between the tables, making sure that everyone was eating tidily and not making a mess. Hamish Bigmore was being unusually nice to him. 'Oh, Mr Magic,' he kept saying, 'isn't it a lovely day? I do hope you're feeling well today?'

'Yes, thank you, Hamish,' said Mr Majeika, obviously pleased that Hamish was being polite.

'Is there anything I can get you?' Hamish asked, smiling sweetly. 'I'm sure the dinner-ladies would give me a cup of tea for you if I asked them nicely. Shall I go to the kitchen and see?'

Mr Majeika smiled back at Hamish. 'That's very kind of you,' he said. 'Yes, I would love a cup of tea if they can make me one without too much trouble.' And off went Hamish.

A few minutes later he came back, carrying the tea. 'Here you are, Mr Magic,' he said, still smiling sweetly. 'I do hope you like it.'

'Thank you, Hamish,' said Mr Majeika, putting it down on the table to let it cool before drinking it.

At this moment Mr Potter bustled up. 'Ah, Mr Majeika, I wonder if we could do a bit of a change-round this afternoon? I haven't seen much of Class Three this term, so I'd like to take them after lunch, and you can take Class Four, whom I'd normally be teaching. Will that be all right?'

'Certainly,' said Mr Majeika.

'That's fine,' said Mr Potter, and he was just going when he saw the cup of tea. 'Ah,' he said, rather puzzled. 'I see the dinner-ladies have left my tea out here today. I always have a cup of tea after lunch, you know. Wakes me up!' And with that, he downed the tea at one gulp, muttered 'Far too much sugar,' and hurried back to his office.

Hamish Bigmore had gone rather pale. 'What's the matter?' Pete asked him.

Hamish said nothing. But a moment later, after Mr Majeika had gone off to teach Class Four, he whispered to Pete: 'We're for it now! Really for it!'

'What do you mean?' asked Pete.

'That cup of tea!' said Hamish. 'It was meant for Mr Magic.'

'I know that,' said Pete. 'But I don't think he really minded Mr Potter drinking it.'

'It's not that, you ass,' said Hamish. *'There was flying potion in it.'*

'What?' shouted Pete.

'Ssh!' said Hamish. 'I meant it for Mr Majeika. I thought I'd get my own back for being turned into a frog, so I hid the flying potion and meant to make him drink it all one day when the window was open, and I hoped he'd fly away out of the window and never come back. And now Mr Potter's drunk it instead!'

'Was there a lot in the cup?' asked Pete.

'The whole bottle,' said Hamish gloomily. 'I can't imagine what's going to happen.'

Pete thought for a few moments. Then he said: 'If odd things start to happen to Mr Potter, we'll *all* get into trouble, you can be sure of that. And if he finds out that Mr Magic's flying potion is at the back of it, you can be sure Mr Magic will lose his job, and Class Three will be given an ordinary teacher instead. Now, that may be what *you* want, Hamish Bigmore, but the rest of us certainly don't. So I'm going to warn everyone *not to pay any attention if Mr Potter starts to fly*. It's the only hope . . .'

When Mr Potter arrived to teach Class Three fifteen minutes later, everyone had been warned. They sat silently at their desks, knowing that something very odd was probably going to happen, but determined not to laugh or give any other sign that something extraordinary was going on.

In fact, for a very long time nothing happened at all. Mr Potter began to give them an ordinary, boring lesson, and the afternoon dragged by as slowly as usual.

'It takes half an hour to work,' Jody whispered to Thomas. 'The flying potion, I mean.'

'The half hour was up a long time ago,' whispered Thomas. 'I can't think why nothing's happening.'

'*I* know,' whispered Pete. 'It's because he's not *thinking* about flying. You've got to think about it in order to leave the ground.'

'Well, let's hope he *doesn't* think about it,' whispered Pandora.

Mr Potter glanced up irritably. 'Stop that

whispering at the back!' he said. 'Have any of you been listening to me? What have I been talking about, Jody?'

There was an awkward silence as Jody tried to remember what Mr Potter had been saying. 'It was something about how the wind works, wasn't it?' she asked hopefully.

'Certainly not!' spluttered Mr Potter. 'I have been giving you a lesson on the force of gravity. Do you know what gravity is?'

Jody shook her head.

'Oh, really!' said Mr Potter. 'You haven't been listening at all. Gravity is the thing which keeps us all on the ground, and stops us floating up *into the air . . .*'

His voice became a squeak of surprise on these last three words, for as he spoke them, he himself left the floor and began to rise slowly towards the ceiling.

There were a few snufflings among Class
Three as they stuffed handkerchieves into
their mouths to stop themselves laughing.
But otherwise, silence.

Mr Potter had stopped rising, and was
suspended in mid-air, about four feet from
the floor, 'Er,' he said, 'something peculiar
seems to have . . .' He looked at Class Three,
and Class Three looked back at him. No one
laughed or said anything. Slowly, Mr Potter
came down to the ground.

'He must have stopped thinking about floating,' whispered Jody. 'Let's make him talk about something else. That should keep his mind off it.'

'Mr Potter,' said Thomas loudly, 'we don't really want to hear any more about the force of gravity. Why not tell us about winds instead?'

'Certainly not!' said Mr Potter crossly. 'Kindly attend to the lesson. As I was saying, gravity stops us from floating in the air. Now you may ask how it is that birds manage to fly? Let me tell you. When birds wave their wings –' He started to wave his arms to show them what he meant; and, as he did so, he rose once more in the air. At first he didn't seem to notice, and simply went on talking.

'By moving their wings,' he said, 'birds create a current of air which permits them to fly wherever they want. They can fly to the left' (and so saying, Mr Potter flew across the classroom) 'or to the right' (he flew back to his desk) 'or round and round in circles.'

As he said these last words, Mr Potter slowly circled the room, and then returned to his desk. He looked puzzled. 'Er,' he said, 'I don't know how to put this, boys and girls, but during the last few minutes, while I was talking to you, I had the strange sensation that . . . well, that *I* was flying like a bird. Did you notice anything odd, boys and girls?'

'Oh no,' said Thomas.

'We didn't see a thing,' said Pete.

'You must have imagined it,' said Jody.

'Only,' said Thomas, 'we wish you'd stop thinking about – I mean talking about – flying, and tell us about something else.'

'Listen, boy,' said Mr Potter crossly, 'I am going to finish my lesson on the force of gravity, and I want no more interruptions from you! Now you must understand that, if it were not for the force of gravity, we couldn't simply walk about on two legs. Why, we'd often find ourselves standing on our heads!' And of course, as he said these words, Mr Potter's feet rose a little from the ground and he slowly turned right over in the air, coming to rest standing on his head.

There was silence. 'Are you *sure* nothing peculiar is happening to me, boys and girls?' came Mr Potter's voice from the floor.

'Oh, nothing at all,' said Pandora Green. 'You're just standing by your desk as usual.'

'Oh,' said Mr Potter. 'Oh well . . . I really ought to go and see a doctor about these funny things I keep imagining . . . Still, I must finish the lesson.' He cleared his throat. 'Not only would we often find ourselves standing on our heads,' he continued, 'but without gravity we could simply float out through any open window, sail up into the sky, and never come back.'

And of course, exactly as these words left Mr Potter's lips, he left the floor and began to float, still upside-down, towards the open window.

'Quick!' shouted Pete. 'Someone shut the window, or he'll never be seen again.'

Everyone made a rush for the window. But just at that moment the bell rang for the end of afternoon school; and as it did so, Mr Potter came back to earth with a bump and sat up, rubbing his head.

'Good gracious!' he said. 'What a lot of funny things I have been imagining. Boys and girls, back to your places! I never said you could go yet.'

'The half-hour's up!' whispered Jody. 'The flying potion has worn off. Thank goodness for that!'

The door opened, and in came Mr Majeika. He was holding something in this hand. 'I hope they behaved themselves?' he asked Mr Potter, who nodded rather weakly. 'That's good,' said Mr Majeika. 'I found *this* in the kitchen.' He showed Class Three what was in his hand; it was the empty bottle which had contained the flying potion. 'I just wondered if anyone had been . . . ?' he said, looking at them meaningfully.

Class Three shook their heads.

'Nothing's happened at all, Mr Magic,' said Hamish Bigmore firmly. 'It was just an ordinary lesson. But I think Mr Potter would like a cup of tea to calm his nerves. And no sugar in it this time.'

7. Dental Problems

'Mr Potter wants everyone to clean their teeth very thoroughly tomorrow,' said Mr Majeika to Class Three, one afternoon about a week before the end of term. 'There's a dentist coming to teach you about careful brushing, and how to fight tooth decay, and Mr Potter says he doesn't want everyone's mouths looking and smelling like the insides of old dustbins.'

'Please, Mr Magic, my teeth are *always* clean,' said a voice. It was Melanie.

'Yes, Melanie, I'm sure they are,' said Mr Majeika. 'But not everyone is as careful as you.'

'Melanie's teeth are *clean* all right,' said Hamish Bigmore. 'But look how ugly they are! They stick out all over the place.'

Unfortunately this was quite true. Melanie did have sticking-out teeth. But of course being told this made her cry even louder than usual. 'Boo-hoo! I hate you, Hamish Bigmore, you're *horrid*!' she wailed.

'Don't you call *me* horrid,' answered Hamish. 'Just think how horrid *you* look, with those teeth. In fact you look just like Count Dracula! Melanie's got teeth like a vampire! Ya, horrid old vampire!'

'Be quiet, Hamish Bigmore,' said Mr Majeika. But Hamish, as usual, wouldn't pay any attention. 'Vampire! Vampire!' he shouted. 'Melanie looks like a vampire!'

Mr Majeika suddenly lost his temper. 'I'll show you who's a vampire!' he cried, and pointed a finger at Hamish.

Hamish Bigmore opened his mouth to say something rude – and then stopped, because everyone was suddenly laughing at him. 'Vampire! Vampire!' they were shouting.

'What's got into you, you sillies?' he asked them. But they would only answer: 'Vampire! Vampire!'

'Here,' said Pandora Green, 'take a look at this.' She kept a pocket-mirror in her desk for putting on lipstick, when Mr Majeika wasn't looking. Now she held it up to Hamish Bigmore.

He stared in the mirror, then turned on Mr Majeika. 'Look what you've done, Mr Magic!' he shouted.

It was perfectly true. Hamish Bigmore had suddenly grown vampire's teeth.

They were very long and pointed, and stuck right out of his mouth. Two were especially long and sharp. It was as nasty a sight as anything in the horror films on television.

'Oh dear, oh dear,' Mr Majeika was saying. 'I seem to have done it again. These old spells just come back into my head when I least expect them, and then I say them to myself without thinking, and then hey presto! the damage is done.'

'But surely you know how to take *this* spell off him?' asked Jody. 'It can't be as difficult as the frog.'

Mr Majeika shook his head. 'It's quite an

easy one,' he said. 'In fact you don't need a spell to get rid of the vampire teeth, I remember that. Hamish himself has to *do* something to have his teeth become normal again. But I can't for the life of me think what it is.'

Hamish Bigmore himself had been sitting silently through this. Now he snarled between his vampire teeth: 'Well, if you can't take these teeth away, I'm going to *use* them. I'll be a real vampire and bite you all! And you know what happens when you're bitten by a vampire? You become a vampire yourself! Ha! ha!'

'Don't be silly,' said Mr Majeika. 'You're not a real vampire. You just happen to have grown a set of vampire's teeth. But I can tell you that if you start behaving in a foolish fashion, Hamish Bigmore, you can be sure of one thing – those teeth will never go away.

Just you put a scarf around your face to hide them, and go home quietly, and tell everyone there that you've got toothache, and go straight to bed, and with luck in the morning they'll have gone.'

For once, Hamish Bigmore did as he was told.

But the next morning the vampire teeth were still there. Thomas and Pete could see them the moment Hamish Bigmore came into Class Three and unwrapped the scarf from around his face. 'Whatever did your mum and dad say?' asked Pete.

'They're away,' said Hamish. 'There's an old aunt of mine looking after me, and she's too short-sighted to notice. Mr Magic should go to prison for doing this to me!'

'It was all your own fault,' said Thomas. 'But what is the dentist going to say?'

This was exactly the thought that crossed Mr Majeika's mind when he arrived in the classroom and saw that Hamish's teeth hadn't changed back in the night. 'Oh dear,' he said, 'this is going to be very awkward.'

When the dentist came, it proved to be a lady. Hamish Bigmore had been put in a far corner of the room, in the hope that she would not look at him, but she went carefully round everyone in the class, making them all open their mouths.

'Now,' she said brightly, peering into Thomas's, 'have you been brushing away regularly with Betty Brush and Tommy Toothpaste? You must remember to fight Dan Decay, and Percy Plaque, or horrid old Terry Toothache will come along and make your life a misery.'

'She's treating us as if we were toddlers in the nursery class,' grumbled Jody. But there was nothing anyone could do to stop the lady dentist chattering away in this daft fashion. Finally she got to Hamish Bigmore, who, on Mr Majeika's instructions, had the scarf wrapped tightly around his mouth.

'Who have we here?' she said brightly. Hamish got to his feet and started to make for the door.

'He's not feeling very well,' said Mr Majeika. 'I think he needs to go to the lavatory.'

'Well, he can just wait a minute,' said the lady dentist firmly. 'Let's unwrap that scarf, my little friend, and see what we find beneath. Are Dan Decay and Percy Plaque lurking there, or have you been a good boy and used Betty Brush and Tommy Toothpaste?'

Hamish Bigmore had had enough of this. He pulled the scarf from his face and bared his horried long pointed teeth at the lady dentist.

'No,' he cried. 'I haven't been a good boy!

I'm Victor the Vampire and I'm going to drink your blood!'

The lady dentist gave a shrill scream, and rushed from the classroom.

*

'Now really,' said Mr Majeika to Hamish Bigmore when order had been restored, 'that was *not* necessary. You might have given her a heart attack.' As it was, the lady dentist had driven away very fast in her little car, saying she never wanted to look at schoolchildren's teeth again.

'I'm sorry you've still got those teeth,' continued Mr Majeika to Hamish, 'but really, behaving so naughtily won't help. I'm still trying to find out what it is you must do to get rid of them – I've been looking through all my old spell-books – and in the meantime I advise you to be as good as possible . . .' Suddenly he stopped.

'What's the matter?' asked Jody.

'I've just remembered!' cried Mr Majeika in delight. 'I've remembered what Hamish has to do to get rid of those teeth! *He has to be good!*'

8. Hamish the Good

At first no one could believe it was as simple as that. But in the end Mr Majeika convinced them all. 'I've remembered what I was taught as an apprentice wizard,' he said. 'If anyone gets a horrid affliction or disease as a result of behaving nastily to someone,' he said, 'they have to be *good* for a certain period of time, and it will go away. So Hamish will have to be good until – well, I should think until the end of term should just about do it. What do you think about that, Hamish?'

Hamish Bigmore looked at Mr Majeika gloomily. 'Isn't there an easier way?' he said.

Mr Majeika shook his head. 'I'm afraid not,' he said. 'For the next week or so, Hamish, you will have to behave like an entirely different person. You must become utterly and completely *good*.'

Hamish sat in silence, stunned by this news.

'He'll never manage it,' said Pete to Thomas. 'Not a hope.'

*

But the surprising thing was that, by next day, Hamish obviously *was* managing it.

Up to now, he had always arrived late at school in the morning, with some silly excuse he'd dreamt up. But today Class Three found him already sitting at his desk when they arrived. And when Mr Majeika came into the classroom, he saw that there was a bunch of wild flowers in a jam jar on his table. 'Oh,' he said. 'Did one of the girls put this here?'

There was a general shaking of heads, and Hamish spoke up: 'No, sir' (he had never called Mr Majeika or any of the other teachers 'sir' before), 'it was me, sir. I picked them from the hedgerow on my way to school. Don't you think they're pretty, sir?'

Mr Majeika looked at Hamish Bigmore suspiciously. 'Don't overdo it, Hamish,' he said warningly. 'Just being *normally* good, like everyone else, will be quite enough.' But Hamish said nothing.

They began lessons. Normally Hamish Bigmore interrupted Mr Majeika at least once every five minutes, with some silly question or rude comment. But today he was completely silent. Mr Majeika obviously couldn't believe it, for he kept casting uneasy glances in Hamish's direction to make sure he wasn't up to something nasty. But not at all. Hamish was very hard at work, and at the end of the lesson he handed a neatly written workbook to Mr Majeika. Class Three had been asked to write something describing a scene in the country, and Hamish's piece was all about sweet little buttercups, and little woolly lambs jumping about in the meadows. 'Are you trying to pull my leg, Hamish Bigmore?' said Mr Majeika. But once again Hamish made no reply.

It was the same at dinner time. Mr Majeika had explained to Mr Potter and the rest of the school that something peculiar had happened to Hamish's teeth, but they would soon be all right again providing nobody took any notice; so Hamish was allowed to have school dinner with everyone else. Usually he fooled around like mad at dinner time, and made a dreadful nuisance of himself to the dinner-ladies. But today everything was different. He not only ate his own dinner as quietly as a mouse, but after it was finished he began to collect up all the other children's dirty plates, knives, forks, and spoons, saying to the dinner-ladies: 'Oh, *do* let me help! Please, is there anything I can do?'

After a bit, one of the dinner-ladies went to Mr Majeika to complain. 'That boy from your class,' she said, 'is giving us all the creeps.'

'Do you mean his teeth?' asked Mr Majeika.

'No, he can't help those, poor dear,' said the dinner-lady. 'I mean his *interference*. He doesn't mean to be a nuisance, the poor creature, but he keeps fussing round us, trying to *help* all the time, and we can't get the washing-up done. What's wrong with him? The other kids never behave like that.'

Mr Majeika sighed. 'I'm afraid he's

suffering from an attack of being good,' he said.

Nor was this the end of Hamish Bigmore's 'helping'. At the end of afternoon school he hurried round to the nursery class, and was soon to be seen 'helping' the little children on with their coats, and holding the door open for the mothers who had come to collect them. Unfortunately nobody in the nursery had been told about Hamish Bigmore's vampire teeth, and the air was soon filled with the screams of terrified mothers. 'It's Dracula himself, risen from the grave!' cried one of the more highly-strung ladies. Mr Majeika, summoned to the disturbance, told Hamish Bigmore to stop 'helping', and to go home at once, but the damage was done, and it was several days before some of the mothers would venture out of doors again with their toddlers.

Every day for a week, Hamish Bigmore thought of some new way of 'helping' someone at St Barty's, and by the end of the week everyone in the school was a nervous wreck. Everyone, that is, except Mr Potter. Somehow Hamish's good deeds had failed to cause any trouble to the head teacher.

On the last morning of term, Hamish Bigmore arrived at school with his teeth looking perfectly normal again. And there was a gleam in his eye. 'Well, I think I've managed it,' he said to Pete and Thomas.

'Your teeth?' they said. 'Yes, you have. They look quite ordinary again. Mr Majeika was right, then – it worked.'

'No, not *that*, idiots,' said Hamish Bigmore scornfully. And his 'goodness' seemed to have vanished now that his teeth were back to normal. 'Just you wait and see what I mean.'

The day ended with the whole school gathered in the assembly hall to listen to Mr Potter. 'I want you all to enjoy your holidays,' he said. 'But before you go, there's one last thing. Those of you who have been at St Barty's for some time will know that on the last day of the Easter term I always give a prize, the Headmaster's Medal for Good Conduct. And as you may also know, beside the medal there's also ten pounds in cash for the boy or girl who wins it. Each year I look for one boy or girl whose behaviour has been really good, and who has tried to be a real help to everyone at the school. And this term, I have no hesitation in awarding the prize to – Hamish Bigmore.'

There was a gasp of surprise and, especially from Class Three, a howl of rage.

'So *that's* what he was up to,' gasped Pete. 'He didn't care about the teeth at all –

he just wanted the money! Well of all
the –'

'Jolly well done, Hamish Bigmore,' said Mr
Potter, hanging the medal round Hamish's
neck and giving him an envelope containing
the money.

'Thank you, *sir*,' said Hamish Bigmore.
And he stuck out his tongue at Class Three.

After it was all over, everyone crowded
round Mr Majeika. 'Wasn't that wicked of
Hamish Bigmore?' Jody asked him. 'Did you
know what he was up to?'

Mr Majeika shook his head. 'I'd never heard of this Good Conduct Medal,' he said, 'or I might have guessed. Why, for two pins I'd turn that medal into a toad!'

'Oh, go on, Mr Magic, please do!' they all said. But he shook his head.

'No, my friends. No more magic, at least not this term.'

'Will you be here *next* term, Mr Magic?' Jody asked excitedly.

Mr Majeika nodded.

'Hooray!' they all said. And then Thomas added as an afterthought:

'Well, don't let Hamish Bigmore ever be *good* again. It's more than we can bear!'

Mr Majeika

Mr Majeika
and the Lost Spell Book

Contents

Contents

1. Mr Potter's Rules

'Now, children,' said Mr Potter, the head teacher of St Barty's School, at morning Assembly, 'tonight – as I'm sure all of you know – is Halloween.'

Everyone felt very excited when he said that, because Halloween was one of the most special days of the year. Maybe even more exciting than Christmas, because you could dress up as witches and wizards, and have lots of fun.

'This year,' Mr Potter went on, 'I am going to make some rules for Halloween.'

Jody and the twins, Thomas and Pete, who were all in Class Three together, looked gloomily at each other. Halloween wasn't the sort of time that you wanted rules. It was all about having fun.

'We need to protect the good name of the school,' said Mr Potter. 'I don't want people to say that children from St Barty's behave badly on Halloween. So here are the rules. You mustn't frighten old ladies. You mustn't wear masks that cover your whole face, because it's very frightening for old ladies – and old men – to open the front door and see people in terrifying disguises. You must only wear little masks that cover your eyes. Don't say "trick or treat" when people open the door, because I don't want you to play tricks on anyone, even if they don't give you sweets. And if they do give you treats, you must say thank you very politely. Please remember these rules. I shall get very cross if people don't keep them. Now you can go to your classrooms.'

'That spoils everything,' said Thomas to Pete and Jody, as they were walking across the playground to Class Three.

'Oh, I don't know,' said Jody. 'We can still have a lot of fun, even if we keep Mr Potter's rules.'

'I'm sure Hamish Bigmore wouldn't agree with you, Jody,' said Thomas. 'And where is he? I didn't see him in Assembly this morning. It's not like him to be late for school, even though he is the worst-behaved boy in Class Three.'

'I reckon we should forget all about Halloween,' said Pete gloomily. 'Something always goes wrong during it. Do you remember the year that all three of us dressed up as ghosts?'

'Oh, that was fun,' said Jody. 'Your mum made us lovely ghost costumes out of old sheets, with holes cut for our eyes.'

'Yes,' said Thomas, 'but we couldn't see out of them properly, and don't you remember what happened?'

'We went to Mr Potter's house,' said Pete, 'and when we tried to find our way up the path to his front door, we got completely lost and fell into his pond.'

'We were covered in slime,' said Thomas. 'Yuck!'

'I've got an idea,' said Jody. 'We could keep Mr Potter's rules, and still have an exciting time. Guess what my idea is!'

'Is it something to do with Mr Majeika?' asked Pete. Mr Majeika was Class Three's teacher. Before he came to St Barty's, he had been a wizard, and he still did magic spells sometimes, though he wasn't supposed to.

'Yes, it is,' said Jody. 'Look, here he comes now. Mr Majeika, could you help us with Halloween?'

'What's Halloween?' asked Mr Majeika. He still didn't know lots of things about ordinary life on earth, because he'd been a wizard somewhere up in the sky, or wherever it was that wizards came from, for a very long time, and he'd only been a teacher for a little while.

'Halloween happens once a year,' said Thomas, 'and it's very exciting, because we all dress up as witches and wizards and ghosts and other scary things like that, and knock on people's doors.'

'And when they open them,' said Pete, 'we say, "Trick or treat?"'

'And if they say "Treat",' said Jody, 'it means they're going to give us sweets, or bars of chocolate, or some other nice thing.'

'But if they say "Trick", it means they'd rather we play a trick on them, like dangling a rubber spider in their face,' Thomas explained.

'That's interesting,' said Mr Majeika. 'In the land of the wizards, we have a night like that. It's called Ordinary People Night, and we all dress up as ordinary people. We stop wearing our wizard and witch hats and cloaks, and put on trousers and shirts and dresses and things – the sort of clothes that you wear down here on earth. And we stop doing spells and magic, and do things like going to school, or to ordinary jobs.'

'It doesn't sound very exciting, Mr Majeika,' said Pete.

'Oh, but it is,' said Mr Majeika. 'It's a great change from spending our days and nights doing magic.'

'We wanted to ask you to help us, Mr Majeika,' said Jody. 'You see, Mr Potter won't let us wear exciting costumes and masks for Halloween tonight. So I was wondering if you could help us by doing a bit of magic.'

'What sort of magic?' asked Mr Majeika. 'You know I'm not supposed to do any at all. That was what the Chief Wizard told me when he sent me down to earth to be a teacher. "Remember, Majeika," he said to me, "not the slightest bit of magic! You mustn't even open your spell book, or wave your magic wand, otherwise there will be dreadful trouble."'

'Yes, but you *have* done magic, quite often, Mr Majeika, since you became a teacher,' said Thomas.

'Almost as soon as you arrived at St Barty's,' said Pete, 'you started doing magic. Surely you remember the time when you turned Hamish Bigmore into a frog?'

'And there have been lots of times since then,' said Jody. 'I don't think that more than a week has gone by without you doing some sort of magic in Class Three.'

Mr Majeika gave a shudder. 'Please don't remind me!' he said. 'If the Chief Wizard knew only half of all the magic

I've done since I came here, I would be in dreadful trouble.'

'What sort of trouble?' asked Thomas. But before Mr Majeika had time to answer, there was a horrible cackling noise from the passage outside Class Three.

'Fee, fi, fo, fum,' chanted a voice, 'I will bite you on the bum! I'll sink my teeth into anyone weaker, especially the neck of Mr Majeika!' The door opened, and in burst Count Dracula.

At least, for a moment they thought it really was Dracula. Then they realized it was just Hamish Bigmore, in a very expensive Dracula costume.

'Are you going to wear that for Halloween tonight, Hamish?' said Jody. 'Because I don't think Mr Potter will like it at all. He told us that we mustn't wear anything that might frighten people.'

'Silly old Piggy-face Potter,' said
Hamish. 'Who cares what he thinks?'

'Now, Hamish,' said Mr Majeika,
'you're not to speak of Mr Potter like
that.'

'Mr Majeika is being very kind,' said
Pete. 'He's agreed to use a little magic to
give us a more exciting Halloween.'

'He hasn't agreed to do it yet,' said Jody.

'But I'm sure he will if we ask him really nicely.'

'Well,' said Mr Majeika, 'I'm sure a *little* magic can't do any harm, especially on an evening when everyone is dressed up as witches and wizards and ghosts.'

'Oh, thank you, Mr Majeika,' said Thomas. 'It will make all the difference to our Halloween.'

'Yes, thank you, Mr Majeika,' said Hamish Bigmore, with a nasty smile. 'Thank you very much.' And he went out of the classroom to take off his Dracula costume in the boys' changing room.

'That's very odd,' said Jody. 'I've never heard Hamish saying thank you before, especially to Mr Majeika. I'm sure he's up to something.'

2. Cousin Lulubelle

At half past six that evening, they all met outside the school gates, wearing their Halloween costumes. Jodie had come as a green-faced witch; her hat and cloak were green as well. 'My mum made my costume,' she said to Thomas and Pete, 'and she found some green make-up for my face. It looks good, doesn't it?'

'Oh yes, very good,' said Pete, though actually he thought it was rather a dull costume. He and Thomas had come all in black, with pointed wizards' hats that had silver stars and moons stuck on them.

'I like your hats,' said Jody, though actually she thought that they looked dull too.

Everyone else had done their best with their costumes, but nobody's was really exciting. One or two people had dressed up as skeletons or ghosts, but it all looked rather feeble. 'I wonder what Hamish will do,' said Thomas. 'Do you think he will pay no attention to what Mr Potter said, and come in his Dracula costume?'

Just at that moment, a big shiny car drew up at the school gates. The driver was a woman, and in the front passenger seat sat Hamish Bigmore. He wound down the window and called out, 'Hi there, everyone!'

'What's he doing in that car?' wondered Pete. 'It's not his mum and dad's.'

Hamish climbed out of the car. They

could see he wasn't wearing any sort of
Halloween costume – he was just in his
ordinary school clothes.

'I want you all to meet my American
cousin,' he said to them. 'Her name is
Lulubelle Bigmore.'

Lulubelle got out of the car. She was a
peculiar shape for a woman, and she had
lots and lots of very bright yellow hair.
From a strap round her neck hung a very
large camera, with an enormous lens.

'Why, hi there, all you little kiddiewinks,' she said in a drawling American accent. 'I hope you don't mind little Hamish's Cousin Lulubelle coming to join in the fun.'

'Er, no,' said Thomas, a bit uncertainly.

'Of course, we have Halloween back home, in old Virginia, where I come from,' said Lulubelle, 'but I reckon all you little British kiddiewinks do things a little differently.'

Just then, Mr Majeika arrived. He had a strange-looking stick with him. It was all sparkly and covered with stars. 'Is that your magic wand, Mr Majeika?' asked Jody. 'We've never seen you use one before.'

Mr Majeika nodded. 'That's right, Jody,' he said. 'I very rarely take it out of its drawer – I don't normally need it to do a spell. But I think tonight is going to be a special night, so I brought it along with me. Now,' he continued, looking around at Class Three and their rather bedraggled costumes, 'let's see what we can do. Everyone must shut their eyes while I find the right spell for the job.'

They all closed their eyes – all except Hamish Bigmore and Cousin Lulubelle. Mr Majeika took a deep breath and then said a lot of very strange words while he waved his left hand in the air, and (with his right hand) pointed his wand at each of them, one by one. For a moment, they all felt a bit peculiar, as if they were being turned upside down and shaken. Then everything seemed normal again, and they opened their eyes.

What they saw was, at first, so frightening that they nearly screamed. Each of Class Three found themselves surrounded by real-life witches, wizards, skeletons and ghosts. It was only when everyone realized that they themselves were a witch, a wizard, a ghost or a skeleton as well that they stopped being frightened, and started to laugh and even cheer.

'Hooray!' shouted Thomas, who had turned into a very funny-looking wizard with a long nose and a big droopy moustache. 'This is the best spell you've ever done, Mr Majeika.'

'I agree,' said Pete, who was a very tall, very thin wizard with knobbly knees, and a beard that came down to his feet.

'Well done, Mr Majeika!' said Jody, who was a short, fat witch – not as nasty to look at as Wilhelmina Worlock, the witch who was always causing trouble for Class Three, but still quite frightening. 'What shall we all do now?'

'Hey, folks,' called out Lulubelle Bigmore, 'you all look great, so smile at the camera, everyone!' And she began to take lots and lots of photos of them.

'Now, everyone,' called out Mr Majeika, 'there's no time to waste – the spell will wear off in an hour from now. So off you go, as quickly as you can.'

'Where should we go, Mr Majeika?' asked Jody.

'Oh, silly me,' said Mr Majeika. 'I quite forgot to give you your broomsticks.'

114

Once again he waved his hand and his wand in the air – and suddenly they all had broomsticks. 'Up into the sky with you,' he said. 'See who can fly the fastest!'

The next hour was the most exciting time that Thomas, Pete, Jody and the rest of Class Three had ever known in their lives. At first they just zoomed around in the sky, learning how to ride on their broomsticks. Then, as they got more confident, they began to fly down to people's houses, where they knocked on the doors and surprised all the people living there, before they zoomed up into the sky again. 'We mustn't go near Mr Potter's house,' warned Jody, and they took care to keep away from it.

Meanwhile, on the ground, Lulubelle was driving her car – with Hamish in the passenger seat – and stopping to take photographs whenever she saw a witch, a wizard, a skeleton or a ghost. She also took lots of pictures of Mr Majeika.

At last, Mr Majeika looked at his watch and called out, 'Time's up!'

One by one, they flew back on their broomsticks to the school gates – though Thomas and Pete couldn't resist having a sky-battle on their way back. Each of them tried to knock the other off his broomstick, until Mr Majeika called to them to stop and behave themselves.

As soon as everyone was back, Mr Majeika lined them up, so that he could do a spell that would change them back into their ordinary selves.

'Hang on there a minute, kiddiewinks,' said Lulubelle Bigmore. 'I want just one more lovely picture of you all and your clever, magical teacher.'

'Do you think we could have copies of the photographs, please?' asked Thomas.

'You bet you can,' said Hamish, with a nasty grin. 'In fact, anyone can get copies of these pictures tomorrow morning just by going down to their newspaper shop. This isn't really my cousin.' And he pulled off Lulubelle's blonde wig, so that they could see that 'Lulubelle' was really a man.

'Allow me to introduce myself,' he said, holding out his hand to Mr Majeika. 'I'm

Dennis Prott of the *Moon* newspaper –
and tomorrow morning you'll all be on
the front page.'

'Yes, Mr Majeika,' said Hamish
Bigmore, very nastily. 'You're in real
trouble now!'

3. The Governors Decide

Thomas and Pete found it very difficult to sleep that night. Early the next morning, they went down the road to the newspaper shop. Sure enough, the headline on the front page of the *Moon* was: 'WOULD YOU WANT YOUR KIDS TAUGHT BY THIS MAN?' The picture showed Mr Majeika waving his magic wand. Beneath it were these words:

'Ace reporter of the *Moon*, Dennis Prott, has discovered WITCHCRAFT being taught to LITTLE CHILDREN in one of Britain's most innocent-looking SCHOOLS. He watched while evil sorcerer Mr Majeika waved his MAGIC WAND and chanted FOUL SPELLS over the CHILDREN, turning them into VICIOUS-LOOKING WITCHES AND WIZARDS. He listened while Mr Majeika taught his VICTIMS to play NASTY TRICKS on OLD LADIES. He gasped in amazement while this WICKED WIZARD passed on to the children the SECRETS of his BLACK ART.

'The *Moon* asks, HOW LONG CAN THIS BE ALLOWED TO GO ON? The *Moon* says, NOT A DAY, NOT AN HOUR LONGER. The *Moon* demands, SACK MR MAJEIKA NOW!!!'

'Oh dear,' sighed Thomas, 'it's even worse than we expected. What do you think we should do?'

They went home and phoned Jody. She had already seen the *Moon*. 'Do you think we should phone Mr Majeika and warn him, before he gets to school?' she asked.

'That's a good idea,' said Pete. 'But does anyone know his home telephone number?'

'I wouldn't bet that he's even got a telephone,' said Jody. 'He doesn't seem the sort of person who would.'

'Maybe we could get in touch with him by telepathy,' said Thomas.

'By what?' asked Pete.

'Telepathy,' said Thomas. 'It's when somebody thinks something, and they manage to make somebody else know what they're thinking.'

'Oh, don't be stupid,' said Jody on the phone. 'You're just wasting time – it can't possibly work.'

'You never know,' said Thomas. 'It

won't take a moment to try it. Let's
practise before we try to contact Mr
Majeika. I'll think hard,' he said to Pete,
'and you've got to tell me what I'm
thinking about.'

Thomas thought hard. He thought
about a car – a big, red, shiny sports car.
In his imagination, he thought about
himself driving it very fast, at a hundred
miles an hour. The car had its roof folded
down, so that the wind was roaring
through Thomas's hair. He was having a
wonderful time.

'What was I thinking about?' he asked
Pete.

'You were thinking about eating a
banana,' said Pete.

Thomas was very disappointed. 'It
didn't work,' he told Jody down the
telephone.

'We *must* stop wasting time,' Jody said.

'Let's get to school as quickly as possible, so that we can try to keep Mr Majeika out of trouble.'

They hurried off to school. As soon as they got there, they saw a big crowd of men and women around the gates. All were holding cameras, microphones or notebooks. And in the middle of them were Dennis Prott and Hamish Bigmore.

'Hi there, kiddiewinks,' said Dennis in

his Lulubelle voice. 'Look at all the friends I've brought with me today. They're all waiting to talk to your naughty teacher – he's going to be on lots of radio and TV programmes, and in all the other newspapers.'

'That's nice,' said Thomas.

'No, it isn't,' said Jody. 'He's going to get into awful trouble – it's the worst thing that Hamish Bigmore has ever done to him.'

Hamish grinned nastily at Jody, and waved Dennis's 'Lulubelle' wig in the air. Pete grabbed it from him, and tried to tear it in half. Then he changed his mind, and ran off with it, calling to Thomas and Jody to follow him.

'Listen,' he said, when they had caught up with him, 'I've got an idea. If we can find Mr Majeika and stop him before –'

'Here I am,' said Mr Majeika. He was

walking past them on his way to school. 'What a lovely sunny morning it is,' he said cheerfully.

'It may be sunny,' said Jody, 'but it's not lovely at all, Mr Majeika, at least not for us.' And she explained to him what had happened.

Five minutes later, they put Pete's idea into action.

Pete pushed through the crowd of reporters and TV and radio people and shouted rude things at Hamish Bigmore, until Hamish lost his temper and tried to hit Pete, who ran away. Hamish ran after him. This was what Pete had wanted – it was important to get Hamish out of the way before his plan could be carried out.

Then Thomas and Jody walked up to the crowd at the school gates, with a third person walking between them.

'Let us through, please,' said Jody. 'This

is our dinner lady, Mrs Maggs, and she's
not feeling very well this morning.'

The reporters and TV and radio people
let them through, but Dennis Prott had a
suspicious look on his face, so they
hurried across the playground as quickly
as possible, and in through the main door
of the school. Too quickly, because Mr
Potter was just inside the door and he
bumped straight into 'Mrs Maggs', whose

hair fell off – because she was, of course, Mr Majeika, disguised in Dennis Prott's Lulubelle wig. Fortunately, the reporters couldn't see what was happening indoors.

'Ah, Majeika,' said Mr Potter, 'I was just looking for you. The governors of the school are holding a special meeting and they want you to come to it.'

'Can we come too, Mr Potter?' asked Jody.

Mr Potter shook his head and led Mr Majeika off by the arm.

'It's all right,' said Pete. 'They're meeting in Mr Potter's office, which is next door to Class Three, and if you go into the big cupboard in the classroom, there's a hole in the wall, and you can see and hear what's being said in the office.'

They hurried into the classroom. There was only room for one person in the cupboard, so Jody went into it and told the others what she could see and hear through the hole.

'There are just two governors,' she said in a whisper. 'One of them is a very old man with a long beard, who seems to be asleep, and the other is – oh no! – it's Hamish Bigmore's mum!'

'What's she doing in there?' said Thomas.

'She became a school governor last term,' said Pete.

'Shh!' said Jody. 'Mr Potter is introducing Mr Majeika to the old man, who's fallen fast asleep again already. And now Mr Potter is reading out bits from the *Moon* about Mr Majeika doing magic, and Mr Majeika is looking very unhappy. Mrs Bigmore is getting very angry and saying that Mr Potter ought to sack Mr Majeika right away. And now –

oh, bother – Mr Potter has taken off his
jacket, and hung it on a hook just above
the hole in the wall, and I can't see or hear
anything any more. We'll just have to wait
until Mr Majeika comes out.

They had to wait for a long while, and
when Mr Majeika finally came into Class

Three, he looked very miserable.

'Have you been given the sack, Mr Majeika?' asked Thomas.

Mr Majeika shook his head. 'Not quite,' he answered. 'Mrs Bigmore wanted Mr Potter to fire me at once, but instead he's told me that I can go on teaching if I promise to give up all magic. So I've promised that I'll break my magic wand, and burn my spell book.'

'That's terrible, Mr Majeika,' said Jody. 'Worse than the sack.'

Mr Majeika nodded. 'It means I can never be a wizard again, for the rest of my life. And I've promised to do it right away.' He took his wand out of the drawer, shut his eyes and bent the wand double, so that Jody, Thomas and Pete were certain it would break. But instead, it vanished!

'Oh dear,' said Mr Majeika, 'I must have

said a vanishing spell over it by accident.'

'Well, you *tried* to break it, Mr Majeika,' said Jody.

'I suppose so,' said Mr Majeika anxiously. 'But I'll have to make sure my spell book really does catch on fire. Here it is,' he said, pulling it out from its hiding place under his desk. 'Has anyone got a box of matches?'

Nobody had. 'Surely, Mr Majeika,' said Jody, 'you could do a fire spell to make it burn?'

Mr Majeika nodded. 'That's a good idea,' he said. He shut his eyes and waved his hands over the book.

Just at that moment, Hamish Bigmore barged noisily into the classroom. 'Yah, boo, sucks!' he shouted at Mr Majeika. 'You'll never be able to turn me into anything again, now that you've had to give up doing magic. Serves you right,

silly old Mr Majeika.' Then suddenly
Hamish yelled 'Ouch!' because the spell
book had risen up in the air, and come
down on top of him with a big thump.

'Oh dear,' said Mr Majeika, 'I didn't
mean to do that at all – I must have used
the wrong spell again.'

The book went on thumping Hamish, and when he tried to run away, it chased him round the classroom. At this moment, the door opened, and in came Mrs Bigmore, followed by Mr Potter.

'What is going on?' shrieked Mrs Bigmore.

'He's done another of his spells,' yelled Hamish, who was trying to hide from the spell book by squeezing under one of the desks. The book found him there quickly, and began to smack him on the bottom. 'Ow! Ow!' shrieked Hamish.

'That proves it!' said Mrs Bigmore. 'Mr Majeika obviously doesn't have the slightest intention of giving up magic. He's going to go on doing horrid magical things to my poor little Hamish. Sack him at once, Mr Potter! Sack him right now!'

Mr Potter nodded gloomily. 'I'm afraid

you're right,' he said to Mrs Bigmore.
'Mr Majeika, you must leave the school
at once, and never come back.'

4. What a Week

A week later, Thomas and Pete were walking home from school with Jody.

'What a dull week it's been,' said Pete. 'I knew that Mr Majeika's magic made school more exciting, but I never dreamed that school without magic could be so boring.'

'Well,' said Jody, 'we haven't been very lucky with teachers, have we?'

There had been a different teacher on each of the five days. On Monday, there had been an old man with a white moustache, who had shouted at them as if they were soldiers in the army under his command. But of course Hamish Bigmore had shouted back at him, so he told Mr Potter he wouldn't go on teaching Class Three.

On Tuesday, they were taught by a very fat man, who ate cream buns while they were writing or drawing. Hamish had stolen one of his buns and smeared it all over the drawings that were pinned on the wall, so of course he wouldn't come the next day either.

On Wednesday, there was a young woman with long hair. Hamish had tied her hair to the back of her chair, and by the time Jody and some of the other girls had managed to untie it, she had decided she wouldn't come back again either.

On Thursday, there had been a big tough man, who looked like a footballer and arrived at school in an expensive-looking car. He had managed to keep Hamish under control, but when he left at the end of school he found that Hamish had poured glue into the door-locks of his car, so he couldn't get into it.

And on Friday, no one would come to teach Class Three, so Mr Potter had had

to do it himself, and very boring this had been.

'It was so dull with Mr Potter teaching us,' said Pete, 'that I reckon Hamish Bigmore must have been missing Mr Majeika too.'

'Look,' said Jody, 'there he is!'

'Do you mean Hamish?' asked Thomas.

'No – Mr Majeika!' Jody pointed across the street to the park. Mr Majeika was sitting on one of the benches. He was looking very miserable.

They ran over to him at once. 'What have you been doing all week, Mr Majeika?' Pete asked him.

'I've tried all sorts of different jobs,' he told them. 'I've been a postman, a milkman, a newspaper-delivery man, a gardener and a builder, but I always make silly mistakes and get the sack. When I was a postman, the letters I was carrying

138

all blew away in the wind. When I was a milkman, I tripped over my own feet and dropped all the milk bottles, so that they broke. When I was delivering newspapers, there was a huge shower of rain, which turned all the papers into soggy sludge. When I was a gardener, I pulled up a root and the tree to which it belonged fell on top of me. And when I was a builder, all the scaffolding that I had put up fell down.'

'Poor Mr Majeika,' said Jody. 'You have had a lot of bad luck.'

'Oh, it wasn't luck,' said Mr Majeika. 'It was Wilhelmina Worlock.'

Wilhelmina Worlock was a wicked witch who had made a nuisance of herself to Mr Majeika ever since he had come to St Barty's School.

'You mean,' asked Pete, 'that she blew away the letters, tripped you, made it rain on the newspapers, pulled up the tree and pushed the scaffolding down?'

'Exactly,' said Mr Majeika. 'She was always invisible, but I knew it was her, because I could hear her cackling with laughter whenever things went wrong for me.'

'Couldn't you use magic to stop her, or to get your revenge?' asked Jody.

Mr Majeika shook his head sadly. 'I tried to, but it didn't work. I said the spells, but nothing happened. You see, my spell book vanished after it had finished chasing Hamish, and now when I shut my eyes and wave my hands, nothing magical happens at all.'

'Isn't there any way you can get your magic powers back again?' asked Pete.

Mr Majeika thought for a moment. 'Well,' he said, 'there is one way. But it would be impossible.'

'Tell us about it, Mr Majeika,' said Thomas.

'A long time ago,' said Mr Majeika, 'I was told by another wizard that, if I ever lost my magic powers while in this world, the thing to do would be to find the Old Back Door, which is a secret way into the place where all magic comes from. I asked him where the Old Back Door was, and he didn't know. But he did say that there was a map showing it. He said this map was the oldest in the world, and it was kept in the oldest library in the world. I asked him which was the oldest library in the world, and he told me that – good gracious, how *could* I have forgotten about that?' And suddenly, Mr Majeika was roaring with laughter.

'What is it, Mr Majeika?' asked Jody. 'What's so funny?'

'He told me,' explained Mr Majeika,

'that the oldest library in the world is in St Barty's Castle.'

'St Barty's Castle?' repeated Thomas in amazement. 'But that's just down the road!'

'Exactly,' said Mr Majeika. 'Come along – we can be there in five minutes!'

5. Who Stole the Map?

The castle was a big building near the
railway station, made of old grey stone.
Alongside a notice giving the opening
hours and the ticket prices was a signpost
that said: 'To the Oldest Library in the
World'. They followed the direction in
which the signpost was pointing, and
found themselves at the back of the castle,
where there was a very old-looking door
with the word 'Library' painted on it.
Above a big iron handle were the words
'Please Ring', so Thomas pulled the

handle very hard, and they could hear the jangling of a bell some distance away.

For what seemed like a long time, nothing happened. Then suddenly a flap in the door sprang open, making them all jump, and a face poked through – the face of an old man with a beard.

'Y-y-y-y-yes?' he said very sharply, but with a stammer. 'You r-r-r-r-rang the b-b-b-b-bell?'

'We d-d-d-d-did,' said Thomas, who seemed to have caught the stammer from the old man. 'I mean,' he went on, without a stammer, 'we did. We want to see the map that shows the Old Back – ow!' He ended like this because Pete had just stepped on his toes, to shut him up. Pete thought it wasn't a good idea to mention the Old Back Door just yet.

'We'd like, please, to look at your collection of old maps,' Pete said.

'H-h-h-h-how old?' asked the old man, looking very suspiciously at Pete.

'Oh, very old indeed, please,' said Jody.

'And w-w-w-w-which of you wants to s-s-s-s-see them?' asked the old man, peering around at them all.

'Our teacher, Mr Majeika,' said Thomas, rubbing his foot where Pete had stood on it. 'He needs to see the map, so that he can discover the Old Back – *ow!*' Pete had stepped on his other foot.

'Mr Majeika?' repeated the old man. 'N-n-n-n-now where have I heard or seen that n-n-n-n-name before?' He looked Pete straight in the eye. 'Are *you* Mr Majeika?' he said.

Pete shook his head. 'No,' said the old man, 'I thought you weren't.'

He shifted his gaze to Thomas. 'Are *you* Mr Majeika? No? I thought not.' This time he looked at Jody. 'And *you* d-d-d-d-

definitely aren't Mr Majeika,' he said to
her, 'which leaves – *you*.'

Mr Majeika nodded.

'Yes, I thought so,' said the old man.
'Well,' he said to Mr Majeika, '*you* very d-
d-d-d-definitely *cannot* come into the
library.'

'What about us?' asked Jody.

'Ch-ch-ch-ch-children not allowed,'
snapped the old man, removing his face
and shutting the door-flap with a bang.

Thomas grabbed hold of the bell-handle, and was going to pull it again, but Pete said: 'No – it's no good arguing with someone like that. We need a better plan.' Then he whispered in Thomas and Jody's ears, and they both nodded, so Pete whispered the plan to Mr Majeika, who nodded as well. 'We'll have to go home first, to get the clothes,' said Pete. So off they all went to Thomas and Pete's house.

Half an hour later, a very strange-looking lady was walking along the path that led round the back of the castle, to the library. She was very tall, and bulged in some rather odd places, and she had lots of very bright yellow hair. She reached the library door, and rang the bell.

When the flap opened, and the old man peered out, the lady said, 'How do you do? I am Mrs Lulubelle Prott, and I would like to see your collection of old maps.'

'W-w-w-w-why, certainly, madam,' said the old man, opening the door. Mrs Prott stepped inside, and the old man shut the door behind her. 'D-d-d-d-do you have any particular map in mind?' he asked her.

'Well,' said Pete, because he was the top half of Mrs Prott, 'I'd like to see anything that shows *doors* – and very old ones, please.'

'C-c-c-come with me,' said the old man. He set off down a dark passage, and Mrs Prott tried to follow him, but her bottom half (who was Thomas) couldn't see where he was going, and bumped into the wall, so that Pete nearly fell off his shoulders.

'N-n-n-n-now,' said the old man, stopping by a door which said 'Map

Room', 'it sounds to me as if you need the map that shows the Old Back Door.'

Ten minutes later, Mrs Prott came out of the main door of the library into the open air. Waiting at the front of the castle were Mr Majeika and Jody. 'How did it go?' asked Jody. 'Did he see through your disguise?'

'No,' said Pete, climbing off Thomas's shoulders and removing the Lulubelle wig. 'And we nearly got to see the map.'

'Nearly?' said Jody. 'You mean you didn't see it?'

'I'm afraid not,' said Thomas.

'Did the old man refuse to show it to you?' Jody asked. 'Oh, and by the way, I knew I'd seen him somewhere before, and now I remember where. He's the old man who kept falling asleep in the governors' meeting. That's why he wouldn't let Mr Majeika into the library – he knows all about him.'

'He didn't refuse to show it to us,' said Pete. 'He went to the shelves and took out an old leather-bound folder with "MAP SHOWING WHERE TO FIND THE OLD BACK DOOR" on it in gold lettering. But when he opened the folder, it was empty.'

'He was very surprised and upset,' said Thomas. 'He said that an old lady and her grandson had visited the library earlier today, and had specially asked to see that map. But he couldn't believe they'd stolen it.'

'An old lady and her grandson?' repeated Mr Majeika. 'You don't think that they could really have been –'

'Wilhelmina Worlock and Hamish Bigmore,' said Pete. 'I'm dead certain they were, because in the folder where the map should have been was a tiny scrap of paper, and written on it was: "Tee hee! Got you this time, Majeika. W. W. and H. B."'

'I'm afraid there's no doubt about it, Mr Majeika,' said Thomas. 'Wilhelmina is going to make sure you don't get your magic powers back.'

'Yes,' said Mr Majeika gloomily. 'And another thought occurs to me,' he went on. 'If Wilhelmina and Hamish can find the Old Back Door, and get into the place where all the magic comes from, then

Hamish can get the magic powers that I've lost.'

'You mean …?' asked Jody.

Mr Majeika nodded. 'If we don't get there first,' he said, 'we won't be able to prevent Hamish from becoming a wizard!'

6. Cosy Corner

Just at that moment, Thomas spotted Hamish Bigmore. He was walking past the castle, carrying something big that was wrapped up in brown paper. 'Look!' whispered Thomas. 'There he is – and I bet it's the map he's carrying.'

'Let's capture him,' said Pete, 'and rescue the map.'

'No, not yet,' said Jody. 'First of all, we should discover exactly what he's up to. Don't you think so, Mr Majeika?'

Mr Majeika nodded. 'I'll tell you what,'

he said, 'I'll make us all invisible, and then it will be easy for us to follow Hamish without him spotting us.' He raised his hands as if he was going to do a spell – and then he remembered. 'Oh dear,' he said, 'I keep forgetting that I can't do magic any more.'

'Never mind, Mr Majeika,' said Jody, 'we can follow Hamish just as well without magic, if we do it carefully and make sure he doesn't see us. If we get too close to him, we can hide behind lamp posts and in shop doorways.'

They set off, doing just as Jody had suggested, and soon they had followed Hamish to the edge of the town, where there was a big supermarket with a car park. Thomas, Pete, Jody and Mr Majeika hid behind the cars, and they watched while Hamish amused himself by undoing a stack of supermarket trolleys, and pushing them hard so that they scattered around the car park.

'That's a stupid thing to do,' whispered Thomas. 'It's getting dark, and the cars will bump into the trolleys. Let's go and stop him.'

'No, don't,' whispered Jody. 'Look who's coming!'

A trolley had rolled into the car park without anyone pushing it. After a moment, Thomas realized what Jody meant, because sitting in the trolley and making it roll where she wanted by magic was Wilhelmina Worlock.

She made her trolley roll up silently behind Hamish and bump him on the bottom. He gave a yell and spun round, then saw that it was Wilhelmina.

'Don't you treat me like that!' he snapped. 'Do that again and I'll tear up your precious map into a million pieces.'

'Tee hee!' cackled Wilhelmina. 'Give me the map! I want it back in case that weaselly worm of a wizard Majeika gets his nasty little hands on it, and uses it to find his way to the Old Back Door so he can recover his magic powers. I'm not letting that happen, oh no!' And she tried to snatch the map from Hamish.

He dodged out of her way, and waved the parcel containing the map in the air. 'Why should I give it to you, you silly old bat?' he snapped at Wilhelmina. 'It's not yours – you stole it.'

'And so did *you*, my little Star Pupil,' said Wilhelmina. 'You helped me steal it and if you're not careful, I'll tell the police – ha ha!'

'Ouch!' cried Hamish, because Wilhelmina had waved her arms in the air and a fierce blue burst of what looked like electricity crackled from her hands across to his. He dropped the parcel and, before he could recover, Wilhelmina picked it up.

'Got it!' she snapped. 'I know you wanted to use it to find your own way to the Old Back Door, you slimy little toad, but you shan't! You shan't! Tee hee!' And, sniggering to herself, she made the supermarket trolley zoom up into the air. In a moment, she had vanished into the darkening sky.

'Stupid old bat,' muttered Hamish to himself. 'So she thinks she can stop me, just like that. The silly thing about witches and wizards is that they don't know about modern technology. She's obviously never heard of photocopying.' And from his pocket he took a big piece of folded paper.

'He's photocopied the map,' Jody whispered to Mr Majeika.

'Let's jump out at him, and snatch it from him,' whispered Thomas.

Pete shook his head. 'I don't think so,' he said. 'For all we know, Wilhelmina may be keeping a close eye on Hamish. They may be quarrelling right now, but if we pick a fight with him, she might just come to his rescue. Anyway, I've got another idea. I reckon Hamish photocopied it at a shop near his house – I know the shop myself. Let's go there, just in case.'

'Just in case what?' asked Jody.

'It's only a chance,' said Peter. 'You'll see.'

So they left Hamish to go on with his game of scattering the trolleys around the car park, and hurried off in the direction of his house.

'There it is!' said Pete after a few minutes, pointing at a shop that said: 'COSY CORNER CANDY SHOP – SWEETS, NEWSPAPERS & PHOTOCOPYING'.

He led them into the shop – and then gasped and stopped in his tracks, because behind the counter was the old man with the beard.

'Good evening, young fellow,' said the

old man. 'Can I help you?' He seemed to have lost his stammer.

'Do you work here in the evenings after the library has shut?' Pete asked him.

'Library?' said the old man. 'What library? I work here in this shop all day, young fellow.'

Jody was going to ask him if he was one of the school governors, but she decided to go straight to the point. 'Has there been a boy here today, doing some photocopying?' she asked.

The old man nodded. 'I think you could say so,' he answered. 'In a word, yes.'

'Please could we look through the rubbish bin,' asked Pete, 'to see if he threw away any copies because they didn't come out right?'

The old man nodded again. 'I think I could allow that,' he answered. He pointed to the waste-paper basket that

stood beside the photocopier and
watched while Pete searched through it.
There were lots of bits of paper, but no
sign of a copy of the map.

'It's no use,' said Pete finally to Thomas.
'You were right – we should have jumped
on Hamish and taken it from him.'

'Are you perchance looking for *this*?'

asked the old man, holding up a crumpled sheet of paper. It had written on it: *'Map of Where to Find the Old Back Door – Top Secret'*. 'I saved this copy, which your young friend threw into the bin,' said the old man, 'because I thought that somebody else might be interested in it. There you are, my friends, and I hope you have fun with it.'

Pete took it from him, and said, 'Thank you very much. Are you *sure* you don't work at the library?'

'Perfectly sure,' said the old man. 'Oh, and before you go, don't forget *this*. It belongs with the map.' He handed them a small packet, labelled *'Not to be opened until you reach the First Place'*.

They thanked him again, walked out of the shop and took a close look at the map.

7. Off to the Wedding

'It isn't a map at all!' said Thomas. 'It's just an empty page with two words on it. That old man in the shop has cheated us. I'm going back to complain!' But when they turned round, they saw that the shop had shut, and when they looked through the window there was no sign of the old man.

'Well,' said Mr Majeika, 'I think it's a case of, never mind what we *haven't* got, let's take a closer look at what we *have* got.' He peered closely at the piece of paper and the two words written on it: 'Crown Jewels'.

Mr Majeika repeated them, '"Crown Jewels". Now,' he asked Jody, Thomas and Pete, 'what does that mean?'

'They're the jewels that belong to the Queen,' said Jody. 'I once went to see them.'

'Really?' said Mr Majeika. 'Does the Queen let people come to her house to have a look at them?'

'They're not in Buckingham Palace,' said Pete. 'They're in the Tower of London, and they're *very* heavily guarded.'

'Are we supposed to steal them?' asked Thomas.

Jody shook her head. 'I don't think so,' she said. 'But maybe when we get there, we'll find the Old Back Door.'

'Did you say this Tower was in

London?' asked Mr Majeika. 'We can get there by magic carpet. Oh – I forgot.' And he started to look very miserable.

'It's all right, Mr Majeika,' said Jody. 'We don't need a magic carpet to get there. We can catch a coach – but it's getting late and I think we shouldn't set off until tomorrow morning.'

Thomas and Pete wanted to go to London right away, and even Mr Majeika looked unhappy at the idea of waiting till the next day.

'It's all my fault,' he kept saying. 'If I hadn't been so stupid at Halloween, we wouldn't have had any of this trouble.'

Next morning, they were at the bus station bright and early, and quite soon the coach had dropped them in London, right outside the Tower.

'What a very grim-looking building,' said Mr Majeika. 'Perhaps they'll lock us

up in there if we do anything to the
Queen's jewels.'

'Look!' said Jody, pointing to a sign that
said: '*Please queue here for visits to the
Crown Jewels*'. 'Let's go and see them –
and keep our eyes open for anything
odd.'

'As long as it's not Wilhelmina
Worlock,' said Pete.

They joined the queue, and had to stand
in it for nearly an hour, but finally they
found themselves climbing some steps
into a darkened chamber. In the middle of
it were some big glass cases, heavily
guarded by men in Beefeater uniforms.

The jewels were very beautiful, and
there were several crowns, to be worn by
the Queen at different times.

'Look!' said Jody, pointing at the most
splendid of all the crowns. 'What's that
folded up and lying in the middle of it?'

Pete gazed at it. 'It's a piece of paper,
just like our so-called "map",' he said. He
leant over the glass case as far as he
could, in the hope of reading what was on
it.

'Hoi, my lad, that's not allowed!' said
one of the Beefeaters. 'Behave yourself, or
you'll have to leave.'

'Oh dear,' sighed Mr Majeika. 'In the

old days I could have fetched it by magic. Wait a minute! Who's got that little packet we were given by the old man at the shop?'

'I have,' said Jody, taking it out of her pocket. 'It says, *"Not to be opened until you reach the First Place"*. Do you think this is the First Place?'

Mr Majeika nodded and took a close

look at the little packet. He opened it up. 'There's some powder inside,' he said. 'I think I know what it is. It's magic, of course, so I shouldn't be using it – but *you* can!' And he handed the packet back to Jody, and whispered some instructions in her ear.

Jody nodded. 'I'll do my best,' she whispered back at him. 'Tell me when to do it. Wouldn't it be best to wait until everyone else has gone?' she said, looking around at all the other visitors who had come to see the Crown Jewels.

'It'll probably work,' muttered Mr Majeika. 'Do it now!'

Jody scattered a handful of the magic powder in the air. All at once, everyone froze. Nothing moved, and all the tourists looking at the Crown Jewels, and the Beefeaters, seemed to have been turned to stone.

Amazingly, the glass case containing the crown unlocked itself and swung open. Silently, the piece of paper floated up from the crown, out of the glass case and into Jody's hand.

A few seconds later, everyone unfroze again. The Beefeaters didn't seem to notice that anything odd had happened, and the glass case had locked itself up again. Jody unfolded the new piece of paper. Like the first one, it had just two words on it: 'BBC news'.

'It's a sort of treasure hunt, isn't it, Mr Majeika?' asked Pete, when he had seen what was written on the paper. 'You go to the place it tells you, and when you get there, you pick up the next clue.'

'That's right,' said Mr Majeika. 'But I don't know what it means by "BBC news".'

'It's simple, Mr Majeika,' said Jody.

'We've got to go to the place where they broadcast the BBC television news. I went there once, to be in the audience for a programme, and I know where it is. Come on!'

Just an hour later, they had managed to join a tour of the BBC television studios.

'The next thing we're going to see,' said the guide, 'is a live broadcast of the lunchtime news. In we all go – but no one is to make a sound!'

'Look, Mr Majeika!' murmured Thomas as they tiptoed into the news studio. 'I can see our next piece of paper. It's stuck to the newsreader's desk. Get ready with the "freeze" powder, Jody.'

A red light flashed, and the newsreader picked up her script and started to smile at the camera. Jody threw a handful of the powder in the air, and once again everyone froze. The piece of paper unstuck itself from the desk and floated into Jody's hand. This time the words on it were 'Cup Final'.

'This is going to be a difficult one!' said Thomas, when they had all unfrozen and come out of the news studio. 'Do you know what the Cup Final is, Mr Majeika?'

Mr Majeika shook his head.

'It's the most important of all the football matches,' Pete explained, 'and they're playing it this afternoon. If we hurry, we can get there in time – but we haven't got tickets, so they won't let us in.'

But in the end, the freeze powder did the trick. Jody threw a little more of it in the air as soon as they arrived at the football stadium, and while everyone froze the piece of paper came flying over the stadium roof and into Jody's hand.

'I expect it was stuck to the ball,' said Jody.

The words on it this time were: 'Royal wedding'.

'This is going to be *really* difficult,' said Jody. 'Do you know about the Royal wedding that's happening today in Westminster Abbey?'

They all nodded.

'Well,' said Jody, 'we're supposed to go to it to look for our next clue! And there's only a tiny bit of the freeze powder left. I'm sure it won't work.'

8. The Old Back Door

But the Royal wedding turned out to be
as easy as the Crown Jewels, the BBC
news and the Cup Final. They waited in
the crowd until the royal couple came out
of Westminster Abbey, and sure enough
Jody spotted the piece of paper attached
to the bride's veil. While everyone was
cheering, she threw the last of the freeze
powder in the air, and everyone froze
immediately – even the bells that were
pealing loudly – until the piece of paper
had floated over to Jody.

'I don't believe it,' she said, looking at the two words on it. 'It just says "Class Three". What's that supposed to mean?'

'I think,' said Mr Majeika, 'it means we should go back to school.'

So they did. By the time the coach had brought them home from London, school had ended for the day, so there was no one around to watch Mr Majeika tiptoeing into his old classroom with Jody, Thomas and Pete. The room was empty.

'So what do we do now?' asked Thomas.

At that moment, the door of the big cupboard creaked open, and a voice said, 'Welcome to the Old Back Door.'

It was the old man – the one who had been the school governor, the person in charge of the Oldest Library in the World, and the shopkeeper. Seeing him again, Mr Majeika scratched his head.

'Now why didn't I recognize you before?' he said. Then he turned to Jody, Thomas and Pete. 'This is a very important person,' he told them. 'The Chief Wizard.'

The Chief Wizard bowed to them. 'I've been trying to sort things out since our friend Majeika got himself into trouble, but the rules said that I couldn't make it too easy for him. Yes, this is the Old Back Door, which leads from the ordinary

world into the world of magic.'

'And it's in our very own school, and our very own classroom?' asked Jody.

'Yes,' said the Chief Wizard. 'That's how we wizards knew about St Barty's School and Class Three. We used to peep at you all sometimes through the keyhole. We could see how nice you all were – well, almost all of you – and that's how we decided that you deserved to have a wizard as a teacher.'

'Thank you very much,' said Thomas. 'And now, please can Mr Majeika have his magic powers back?'

The Chief Wizard frowned. 'I'm afraid I've got some bad news,' he said gloomily. 'I knew it might happen as soon as Hamish Bigmore stole the map from the Oldest Library in the World.'

'So you didn't mean to let him steal it?' asked Jody.

The Chief Wizard shook his head. 'Certainly not,' he said. 'I failed to recognize him. We knew that you had a troublemaker in the class, but when he came to the library I didn't realize who he was.'

'So what's the bad news?' asked Jody anxiously.

'Well,' answered the Chief Wizard, 'the rules say that anyone who finds the Old Back Door gets his or her magic powers back, if they've been lost. And if they haven't ever had magic powers, they can get them and become a wizard or a witch. You see, Majeika's magic powers have been waiting here for him to reclaim them. But I'm afraid they have to go to the first person who turns up and asks for them. And I'm very sorry to say that someone else did get here first, before all of you, and he's laid claim to Majeika's magic. Step forward Learner-Wizard Bigmore!'

Jody, Thomas and Pete groaned as, out of the cupboard, there stepped Hamish in a wizard's cloak and hat, with a wand in one hand and a spell book tucked under his other arm.

'Ha ha ha!' he said, in his nastiest voice.

'Now I can *really* get my revenge on you, Mr Majeika.' And he raised his magic wand in the air.

'Wait a minute, Learner-Wizard Bigmore,' said the Chief Wizard. 'First of all, every new wizard has to take a Magic Test, before he can be granted a full wizard's licence.'

Hamish scowled. 'You didn't tell me that,' he grumbled. 'I demand fair treatment!'

Suddenly there was a whooshing noise, and Wilhelmina Worlock flew past the window on her shopping trolley. She landed it in the playground, and hurried into Class Three.

'Is my Star Pupil going to do his Magic Test?' she cackled. 'Take my advice, young Hamish, and look up all the spells in your book before you try them out.'

'Who cares about that stupid old book?'

said Hamish. 'I know how to do all the spells – I've learnt them by watching Mr Majeika, and they're easy-peasy. Any old fool can do them.'

'If it's as easy as you say, Hamish,' remarked the Chief Wizard, 'we won't waste any more time. Let's start right away, with the first question. Learner-Wizard Bigmore, make yourself invisible, so that no one can see you.'

Hamish shut his eyes and muttered some words. They must have been the wrong ones, because he didn't become invisible at all. He turned bright green, and smoke came out of his nose and ears.

'Nought out of ten,' said the Chief Wizard. 'Second question. Learner-Wizard Bigmore, make yourself rise in the air and float above the ground.'

'That's easy-peasy,' said Hamish, and he closed his eyes and muttered a spell

again. This time he almost got it right,
because Thomas, Pete, Jody, Mr Majeika,
the Chief Wizard and Wilhelmina
Worlock all rose up in the air. But Hamish
himself stayed firmly on the ground.

'Minus five,' said the Chief Wizard.
'You get a penalty for doing the right spell
to the wrong people. Now, this is your
last chance, Learner-Wizard Bigmore. For

your third and final question, make
somebody else look like you. I need a
volunteer for this one – Wilhelmina
Worlock, you'll do fine.'

Wilhelmina grumbled like mad, but in
the end she stepped forward and stood
opposite Hamish. He closed his eyes and
muttered a spell – and nothing happened
to Wilhelmina. Hamish, however,
changed completely – into a smaller
version of Miss Worlock, except that on
his head was the 'Lulubelle' blonde wig.

'Nought out of ten,' said the Chief
Wizard. 'Learner-Wizard Bigmore is
herewith deprived of his magic powers.
They revert to Mr Majeika, who becomes
a full wizard again.'

'Do you mean he gets his spell book
back, and he can do magic once more?'
asked Pete, as Thomas and Jody cheered
at the good news.

'That's right,' answered the Chief Wizard. 'Remember, Majeika, you're not *supposed* to do magic at all, now that you're a teacher. But I shan't be watching that closely!' And he gave a wink.

'You stupid idiot!' Wilhelmina Worlock screamed at Hamish Bigmore. 'I'll never call you my Star Pupil again, you brainless little weasel.'

Hamish was tugging at the wig, but it wouldn't come off his head, and he still looked exactly like Miss Worlock. 'I think we'll let him stay like that for a bit, shall we?' said the Chief Wizard. 'Maybe until next Halloween?'